MW01452234

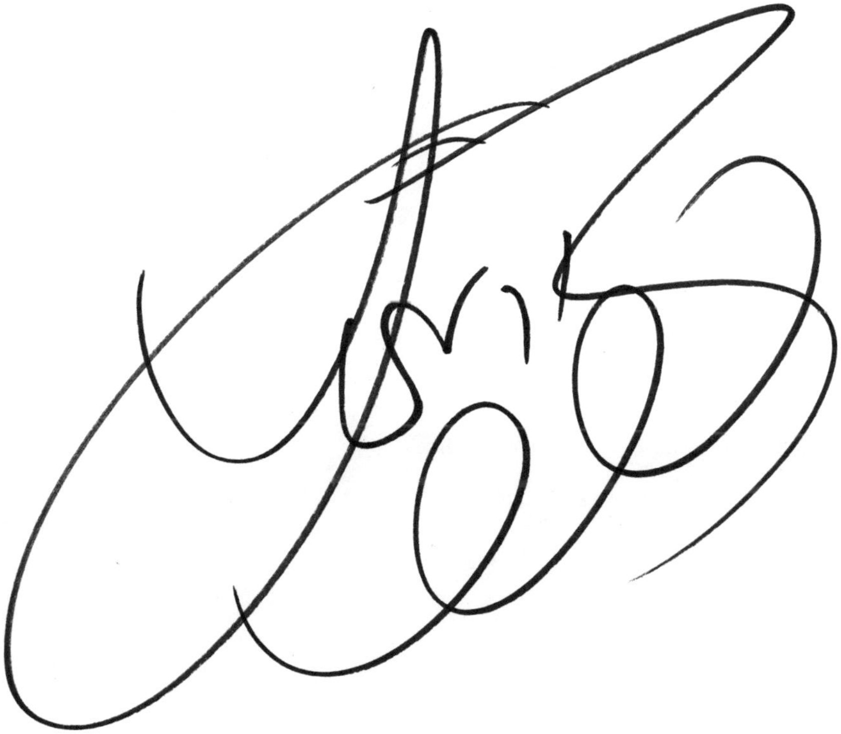

As We Are

Book 2

Stronger than Truth Trilogy

Lori Bell

This book is a work of fiction. Names, characters, places and incidents are the product of the author's imagination or are used fictitiously. Any resemblance to actual events, locales, or persons, living or dead, is coincidental.

Copyright © 2019 by Lori Bell

All rights reserved. This book or any portion thereof may not be reproduced or used in any manner whatsoever without the express written permission of the publisher except for the use of brief quotations in a book review.

Cover photograph by CanStock Photo

Printed by CreateSpace

ISBN 978 1080565696

DEDICATION

To a woman I admired most in this world.
She was beautiful, classy, loyal, and loving.
There will be a void in my heart for the rest of my life now that she's gone.

In loving memory of my grandmother

Shirley Moss

October 6, 1929 — July 20, 2019

Chapter 1

She listened to the repetitive sound of the scissors near her ear as it snipped inches, several inches, off her hair. Cropped in layers and much shorter in the back with a longer, tousled effect on the sides and the top, the style was a modern, chic, pixie cut. Her stylist touched up the stubborn gray hairs with a color that was a close match to her natural caramel brown with sporadic blonde highlights. She may have gone heavier on the blonde this time. Afton Drury studied her new look in the mirror. She hadn't worn her hair remotely short since she was in the third grade when her mother convinced her of how cute it would be. *The mushroom, or bowl cut, wasn't cute then.* Now, at fifty years old, Afton welcomed change into her life. She also was trying to lose a few pounds and tone her body like it once was. *Or maybe she would just get realistically close.* This short haircut —with somewhat of a disheveled, wild style— had the potential to shave years off her age as it swept to the side and close to her eyes. There was already something about this transformation that Afton liked. She hoped the steady love in her life, Knox Manning who was seven years her junior, would like it too.

Afton nonchalantly looked down at her cell phone on her lap at the salon, and she noticed a missed call from her sister, Laney.

Battle Creek Middle School in Saint Paul, Minnesota sometimes felt like a battle ground to Laney Potter. She was an eighth-grade science teacher, always attempting to redirect, guide, and mold hormonal preteens and teenagers into decent human beings. Sure, she wanted them to learn and take away a thing or two from her science lessons and lab experiments, but really what she hoped for the most was for them to make good choices and to show genuine kindness. *Who was she kidding?* Two of those boys in the mix, in the seventh grade, were her own twin sons who recently turned thirteen years old. She and her husband, Brad, were just beginning in the world of parenting oftentimes defiant teenagers. Luke, the jock in both baseball and basketball, was entirely focused on sports. Liam excelled in academics when he applied himself. Lately though, he was more concerned about girls — which Laney feared was only going to get him into trouble. He was her mischievous child. Working at the same school increased her anxiety this year. She warned her sons that if either one of them landed themselves in the principal's office —with her very own boss for crying out loud— they would not survive the embarrassment she would reciprocate. For starters, she would walk them to their first-hour class each morning, and then later sit beside them to eat lunch.

Teachers congregated outside of Laney's closed classroom door. She could see them through the vertical rectangular-shaped window. It was her planning period, and she was tempted to just ignore her sudden curiosity and continue to accomplish something during her free forty-five minutes. A few seconds later, she overruled her own ambition to complete her checklist as she opened her door and interrupted her co-workers. Both were eighth grade teachers just across the hall. They exchanged a peculiar glance between them before Mr. Black spoke. "I just caught a half dozen, well four, boys vaping in the restroom."

Laney's eyes widened. "Seventh or eighth?" *Please ... not one of mine.*

"All seventh."

Laney held her breath and noticed that Ms. Stempel had yet to make eye contact with her since she stepped out into the hallway with them. "Luke or Liam?" She cringed and braced herself to hear *Liam*.

"Just tell her," Ms. Stempel broke her silence, which didn't help Laney feel any less panicked. She had spoken loudly and repeatedly in her household about the dangers of the vaping addiction. She was old-fashioned in the way she believed *loud and clear* could still be effective.

Mr. Black stepped closer to Laney and kept his voice down. "Liam was not one of the boys that I sent to the office," Laney ceased holding her breath, but her relief was premature as Mr. Black had more to share with her. "He was in the restroom though. He either bolted into a stall just in time for me to walk in, or he was innocent. I let him go."

"Thanks Jon," Laney gave him a soft smile. He nodded.

"If you're not going to tell her the rest, I will," Ms. Stempel chimed in again. Laney stared at them.

"There was a JUUL in the stall that Liam came out of." A JUUL was a type of electronic device used for stimulating the experience of smoking a cigarette. The heated liquid generated an aerosol or a vapor that's inhaled. Laney was aware most kids believed that the liquid used in vaping was only water and flavoring, but she had preached to her boys that it did contain toxic chemicals, including nicotine.

Laney felt both anger and disappointment rise in her chest. "I'll take care of this at home. I appreciate knowing, I really do." It just sucked the life out of Laney to be both a mother and a teacher in that school building right now.

After she was back inside her classroom alone, Laney contemplated calling Brad. She needed to calm down, and she also wanted someone else's advice before she confronted her son in a matter of hours. Her husband worked in construction though, so getting ahold of him at a moment's notice was nearly impossible. Instead, but with no luck, she had tried to call her older sister, Afton. She already raised her own children and had been through enough with them to know how to handle what felt like a crisis to Laney right now.

Skye held two-year-old Bella's little hand as she toddled up the driveway of the house on Holly Avenue *where Aunt Afton lived now.*

It wasn't as tense or awkward anymore for Skye to be around Knox. They managed to get past what happened between them once Afton forgave them both. Seeing the two of them together, and especially witnessing Afton's genuine happiness, was everything Skye had wanted for her older sister. Their age difference was ten years and they had never been very close until recently.

Skye held her little girl in her arms as she rang the doorbell. Simultaneously, Afton sent an unseen text to inform her she was running a few minutes late, but on her way. Then the front door to that Victorian house opened and Knox faced her.

"Oh hey, um, Afton's not home yet?"

"She should be on her way," he smiled, focused on Bella in her arms. The man was a little kid magnet. Bella immediately responded to him the very first time they met, and even more so now.

"Knock!" was the toddler's best attempt at pronouncing Knox as her little round face lit up and she never lost any of that mounting excitement when Knox reached his hand in the air to grasp her tiny fist. He glanced at Skye first. She nodded.

"Yes, take her. She obviously wants a squeeze from you." There was a squeal too as Knox moved back from the doorway with Bella in his arms. Skye stepped inside. The heels she had worn to a web design meeting today allowed her to almost meet Knox's six-foot height in bare feet. The length of her skirt was borderline respectable, and her blouse was cut low enough to reveal some cleavage. Knox far from noticed though, as he was entirely engrossed in being the equivalent to a fun uncle. There wasn't a marriage or even an engagement to make him an official member in the Gallant family, but they all knew he'd stick around for life. Skye tried not to let her mind go exactly where it went, but to no avail. *Knox would make a fun-loving father.* But that was not meant to be. Some people never became parents, and many children didn't always have both a mother and a father to raise them. It wasn't a regret for Skye. Not entirely. But there was a void in her child's life, lacking a daddy. Skye only had fleeting relationships. When Bella was a baby it didn't matter as much to Skye. She felt like she was enough for her daughter. But seeing what Knox brought to her little girl's life, during moments like this, had started to make Skye think she should have given her a father.

It was obvious how careful Knox was not to overstep. But his almost instantaneous bond with Bella was impossible to ignore. He entertained her and played so attentively with her every single time their paths crossed. Skye stood with her arms folded across her chest and she was very close to the front door when Afton suddenly opened it.

"Oh you're home!" Afton referred to Knox, who was now down on the floor with her sweet little niece who had the darkest head of hair she had ever seen on a baby and now a toddler. Those genes were not ones of a Gallant girl.

Before Knox could tell Afton that his hospital board meeting was cancelled at Regency Minneapolis, both he and Skye saw her short hair. Skye, being the quickest on her feet, and the loudest, spoke first. "Your hair! Oh my gosh, that look is perfect for you!"

Afton beamed as she reached for and squeezed her sister's hand. And she also caught Knox's eye, while he was looking up at her from down on the floor. His expression was definite approval. Perhaps it was even his most obvious come-hither look that she had been on the receiving end of since the first fiery moment they met. Skye picked up on that as well. She looked away as soon as she saw the exchange between Afton and Knox. Even in shared silence, their chemistry was loud.

Chapter 2

There were a group of teenage boys playing basketball on the driveway, while Laney stood in her kitchen with her back against the sink. She sipped a full glass of Moscato when the door from the garage opened, and her husband came inside. His jeans were dirty, his white t-shirt didn't look bleached anymore. His short-cropped brown hair was matted from perspiration. "Hi there," Brad Potter winked at his wife.

She smiled. "Don't look at me like that until you've stripped and showered."

He laughed. It wasn't unusual for Laney to have a drink before dinner, or while she was cooking. Today, however, she wore a look that told her husband she needed the alcohol.

"Rough day in the classroom?"

"In the hallway… when I found out that our son may or may not have been vaping in the bathroom. He was one of the lucky ones not caught in the act and reprimanded."

"Liam," Brad spoke for clarification.

Laney nodded. "I have not said a word to him yet. I needed to cool down and get your input first."

"Well I'm not happy if it was him," Brad shrugged, "but it could be worse, right? How do we even approach this with him? I mean, come on Lane, you and I smoked our share of Camels in high school."

She suppressed a giggle at the thought. This, however, was not them nearly thirty years ago. This was their teenage son. "But," Laney began her rebuttal, "then, it was cool and we were oblivious to the health risks. Now we are smarter! How many times have you heard me preach the dangers of vaping to the boys? I'm out of words. Beating him is all I can come up with."

Brad laughed out loud again. "He's as tall as you are and probably weighs more. Not a good idea."

"What do you mean probably weighs more?" Laney feigned being offended. She was forty-five years old and still maintained a decent figure. She stood in her kitchen in her after-school clothes, which hardly defined her as being middle age. Faded cut-off denim shorts were frayed on the ends, and a white sleeveless t-shirt showed off her toned arms.

"Definitely does. Is that better?"

"Can we concentrate on Liam?"

"Only if you promise not to make too big a deal of it. He's thirteen. He has a lot of growing up to do yet." Brad was always the first to defend his boys. He was a fun dad. And that was what Laney feared most for their teenage years. Someone had to show some authority. But she didn't want to do it alone. Not with the serious stuff. Like vaping.

Laney stared at him.

"I don't know why you waited for me. You are more than capable of laying down the law on your own."

She didn't know if she should take his words as a compliment or as a copout. She stayed silent as her husband left the kitchen, and headed to the shower. Devoted to each other since they were sixteen and seventeen years old, their love was storybook. Raising their boys together had been a joy. Until now. And Laney feared this was just the beginning of feeling as if she was parenting mostly alone.

"All I'm asking you is, were you vaping in the bathroom before Mr. Black barged in?" Laney brought up that subject at the dinner table. It wasn't impromptu. It was planned. She wanted the truth. Luke was wide-eyed and focused on his brother. He likely already knew if his brother was guilty, or not. Brad was twirling the spaghetti noodles around on his plate with his fork. Obviously, he chose not to participate in this conversation.

"I was in the stall. You can ask him. I came out when he walked in and caught the others," Liam defended himself. Both of her boys had dark brown hair like their father. They were fraternal twins. Liam looked like Brad, and Luke favored Laney. He even had a faint bridge of freckles across his nose like she and her sisters did. And right now, Laney would admit that she preferred parenting Luke over his brother. He was the compliant, easy one.

"That's exactly what Mr. Black told me," Laney began, "but he also said he found this in the stall after you left." Laney placed the JUUL on the tabletop. It had been on her lap and now it was in the middle of their dinner table. Luke stared at it with wide eyes. Liam tried to react like he had never seen it before. "Is it yours, Liam?"

Her son, who was older than his brother by one minute and thirty-three seconds, opened his mouth to speak. But first, Laney interjected. "Before you answer me, I will warn you that if you lie, you will not date until you are sixteen."

Liam creased his brow. "That's three years, mom."

"I am aware of that. That includes taking a date to the school dances too." Laney watched Brad shake his head. He didn't approve of her tactic. And it probably was overboard, but damn it, she wanted the truth. And what did her boy enjoy the most at this age? *Girls.*

"It was mine," she heard her son say.

"Dude, have you not heard mom at all? That stuff is dangerous!" Luke chimed in, and Laney could have thrown her body across the table that separated them, just to hug his neck.

Liam shrugged.

Laney felt her heart rate quicken. Her son was acting callous. She looked at Brad, and his expression had not altered. Nor did he look like he had anything to say. "Who did you get it from?"

"Mom. Seriously? You teach at the school. I'm not ratting anyone out. Just punish me and leave it at that."

"That a boy. Take the consequences like a man," Brad finally chimed in, and Laney watched their son share a smile with him. They may as well have fist bumped each other. They were buddies. And this was not the time for that. Laney was livid.

"I want your cell phone for the rest of the week. You can have it back on the weekend."

"But it's only Tuesday..." Liam tried to object.

"Right, and if you continue to whine about it, I'll keep it until next Tuesday." Liam stood up from the table and reached into the cargo pocket of his khaki shorts. He tossed his phone on the table and it bounced toward Laney's dinner plate.

She held her breath, because she wanted to scream at him. He looked like he was about to storm out of the kitchen. "Sit back down and finish your dinner." Laney managed to speak those words in a calm manner.

The rest of their time as a family of four at the dinner table was silent and awkward.

And later, while alone in their bedroom, Laney had more to say to Brad.

She watched him walk across their bedroom. His cobalt blue boxer shorts hung low on his hips. His body was in shape. His skin was sun-kissed from working outside, and he actually managed to avoid a farmer's tan in most places. His hair was still wet from the shower. He reached up to power on the TV mounted on the wall.

"The remote is over here," Laney said to him, and she pointed to the nightstand on his side of their queen-size sleigh bed. He joined her in bed a moment later. She was on top of the ivory duvet, wearing a pale pink tank top with matching boy-shorts panties. Her caramel brown hair was still pulled up into her after-school messy bun, sprouting wiry loose hairs. "I want to talk to you about Liam."

Brad wore an uninterested look. "Why? You took care of it. I doubt he will try vaping again. I mean, you took away the boy's lifeline for days." Brad left out the fact that he already saw Liam on his brother's cell phone before bedtime tonight. Laney would be fighting mad if she knew.

"It's just a phone. He'll survive."

"Oh yeah? How many times have you been on social media tonight?"

She shrugged. She was just as attached to her cell phone as anyone else. And besides, her sisters had both posted some fun pictures tonight. Afton showed off a new, chic haircut. And Skye had taken a selfie with Bella at the park. "That's irrelevant. I am not the one being punished."

"Are you sure about that? I think you should be spanked…"

Laney rolled her eyes. "Simmer down. I'm not in the mood."

Oh but then he found that spot just below her earlobe. Her entire body tingled just from the tip of his tongue. She immediately tightened in places that only this man had been. He didn't stop and she didn't resist. And that was their story. Their connection ran deep. Their passion knew no boundaries. She loved this man. She desired him beyond words. He was hers. *Imperfections and all.*

Chapter 3

The Gallant sisters sat in Afton's kitchen. She loved her new, but older, home on Holly Avenue. It was built in 1883 and when Knox bought it, he had no idea he would fall in love with a woman who admired the history of it as much as him. Their home had substance, with a tasteful stamp of days gone by on the exterior, and an abundance of history inside those walls. It still had casement windows, a tiled fireplace in the upstairs master bedroom, and an original second staircase hidden behind a hallway closet. That passageway led to the kitchen and had no longer been used for many years. Afton was absolutely fascinated with it. She lured Knox to the stairway before bed one evening. She had candles burning on the steps. It was another intimate encounter between them, as their passion continued to soar to new heights in ways that neither of them ever wanted to lose.

Afton poured a glass of Moscato for each of them. Laney and Skye shared a bench on one side of the rectangular-shaped table tucked into the corner of the kitchen. Afton sat across from them on one of the two dining chairs. "Your haircut..." Laney stated, "I can't get enough of it. It looks adorable on you."

Afton was flattered. "Thank you. It was a bold change, but I don't regret it at all." Skye had noticed quite a few not-so-subtle changes in her big sister as of late. Her clothing style was different. Her V-necks were lower. Her skirts were shorter. None of it was inappropriate. She was just finally a woman sure of herself and her own body. And that, they all knew, had everything to do with the sexy new man she was shacking up with.

"Knox likes it too, doesn't he?" Skye winked. It was okay for her to talk about Knox with Afton. No one thought anything of it anymore. Even if Skye still carried the guilt and remorse from seducing Knox — a man she had no idea had been on the verge of a serious relationship with her sister.

Afton felt her cheeks redden. "He's fond of it, yes."

"He's fond of you," Laney smiled. "We're so thrilled for you. Are you happy? Has living here been a seamless adjustment?"

"Yes," Afton was quick to answer. "It was difficult to leave the home where Sam and I raised our family for twenty-five years. It was harder for the kids to close that chapter than it was for me, to be honest." Afton had been ready to move on, and eager to put many of her memories of her marriage to Sam behind her. She didn't want to live in their house alone. "Knox has been wonderful. And I love that he's willing to share this place with me. It has quickly become ours."

Skye raised her glass and the three sisters toasted to *happiness*. Afton had finally found it. Laney was living it, with a few glitches (but that was real life), and Skye wondered if she would ever truly find and experience it. Her baby girl completed her life in so many special ways. But there was something missing. Although it had taken her decades to realize, Skye longed to find a genuine, lasting love. Her change of heart was Afton's fault. Seeing the way her life had suddenly turned around, once she met a man who rocked her world, was something Skye could not deny she also wanted for herself. *It was never too late.* She was not in love with or infatuated with her sister's man. She was just looking for much of the same in her own life.

"Enough about me. Tell me about the two of you. What's new, good, or not-so-wonderful?" That was why they agreed to meet once a week, for food or drinks, and especially for the time to remain in touch so they would never again have to start from an unsteady place to reconnect with each other.

"Well you both know about Liam," Laney began, as she had separately vented to her sisters about the trouble he found with vaping at school.

"At least he escaped getting caught and punished at school. That's too embarrassing for you, working there and all," Skye spoke.

"It is, but I'm finding out that teenagers are going to embarrass their parents as much as we do them. I just don't know if I'll survive the next several years." Laney sighed.

"You will, because you have to. And let me tell you, it really never ends. I'm still sifting through difficult times with my two and they are in their twenties!" Afton stated, shaking her head at that truth. Her twenty-four-year-old son had newly come out as gay, and her twenty-two-year-old daughter was pregnant and unmarried. Afton had taken their circumstances and life choices in stride. She was making a diligent effort to be a supportive mother to them. And she made no secret of the fact that she was beyond thrilled with the idea of becoming a granny.

"You make it sound like there's more," Skye hinted for Laney to share what was on her mind.

"Oh there is more," Laney spoke as she placed the rim of her wine glass to her lips and took a generous sip. "For years I have made the boys put away their own laundry. I fold it, stack it, or hang it, and they put everything where it belongs in their room. Well, a few days ago I put away their socks and underwear in their dresser drawers."

"You were looking for something," Skye interrupted.

Laney nodded. "I wanted to see if Liam was stashing those freaking JUULS in his bedroom."

"I didn't even know they were called that," Afton interjected, and Skye laughed at her.

"I didn't find one, but I did discover a newfound interest of his," Laney drank more wine, and her sisters listened raptly. "He had a stash of condoms in there."

"Holy shit..." Skye spoke first because that's what she did.

"Geez Lane, wasn't he just twelve years old?" Afton had not said something that Laney wasn't already thinking. Over and over.

"That's what I told Brad. For the love of God, I have only been a mother for a little more than a decade. I am in no way prepared to be a granny!"

Both of her sisters nodded their heads in unison.

"So, you were able to talk to Brad about this?" Skye again beat Afton to a question. They both knew Laney's struggle with being the sole disciplinarian.

"He wasn't at all upset. He was surprised, but as a fellow guy, I think he was a little proud." Laney rolled her eyes. "I wanted to ask Brad to talk to Liam, but I knew that would be a dire mistake, so I confronted my son alone."

"Did he admit to anything?" Skye was both direct and inquisitive.

"He was humiliated and of course angry with me for rummaging through his underwear drawer. Once I got his focus off that, he swore he has not had sex yet. He was only preparing for if, or when, that time comes." Laney finished off the wine in her glass, and before Afton stood up to get her a refill, she asked, "Do you believe him?"

"I want to," she admitted, "but I'm not sure if I do. He's a confident teenage boy. There is nothing awkward or shy about him." Laney paused. "And in recent weeks he's been hanging out, and occasionally taking a drive, with our sixteen-year-old neighbor girl. She's quite the little hottie."

As Afton topped off all of their wine glasses, Skye responded, "I think you have your answer. And now you can preach safe sex in your house too."

"Can we please change the subject, or I'll be asking one of you to drive my drunk-self home tonight." They all giggled.

"Okay Skye, your turn," Afton stated. "How's our little prodigy doing this week?"

"There's not a word she cannot repeat. She comprehends absolutely everything. I swear it's like living with a tiny adult. She's my heart, and already I'm so proud."

"She's definitely something," Laney smiled.

"And how's your love life?" Afton wanted to be the one to ask that question. She needed for Skye to know that she was forgiven for her encounter with Knox. Even though it was still difficult to completely forget.

"You know I'm happy being Bella's mom. I don't need a man to complete me. I'm whole as I am. I really am," Skye repeated. "But, lately, I am finding myself wishing for someone to go on an adventure with. Someone who will dance with me in the kitchen, kiss me just because, and make me laugh over something silly."

Afton reached across the table for Skye's hand, and Laney joined hers with theirs. "Oh honey. He's out there for you. Look at me. Knox pretty much showed up on my doorstep and fell into my lap."

"How did this suddenly turn dirty?" Laney interjected, and the three of them howled with laughter.

Chapter 4

Jess Robertson held a box of tissues in her hand and sympathetically offered it to the woman in her seventies with her middle-aged daughter beside her. Their arms were wrapped around each other. The tears were freefalling.

"Please, take a moment and when you're ready we will all have a seat and go through this slowly. This is hard, and thinking and making any decisions right now seems impossible but that's why we are here to help." Jess glanced behind her at the interim director of Robertson Funeral Home. Patrick Robertson was her late husband's cousin. Until his unexpected death several months ago, Mark Robertson was the man in charge there. He had been a third-generation funeral director and mortician for that funeral home in Saint Paul, Minnesota. Patrick oversaw another Robertson Funeral Home located in the Twin Cities in Minneapolis. In fifteen months, Jess was going to take over the direction of this funeral home when she finished mortuary school. She was currently studying mortuary science and completing her apprenticeship under Patrick's wing. It was a change she needed to make. She shifted careers from being a speech pathologist at Battle Creek Middle School in Saint Paul to becoming a mortician and funeral director. It was a new path in her life that Jess was ready to follow.

Patrick watched her and listened to Jess' every word to the bereaved. They were not just customers for them. These people were sinking in shock and disbelief and they were consumed with grief that truly had not yet affected them in the full sense. His cousin Mark had been a lucky man, he thought to himself. Jess was a beautiful woman. Her long dark hair was halfway down her back, styled in soft, loose curls. She wore a knee-length black pencil skirt and a solid, sleeveless coral blouse. Patrick tried to resume his focus on the job he was supposed to be watching her do. He was training her to take over this business. And he had every ounce of faith in her capabilities. She was smart, compassionate, and she had previously learned a majority of the business from her late husband. But his attraction to her was becoming harder for him to conceal. He had a wife and three children at home, he reminded himself as Jess' words caught his attention.

"You can trust in our promise to take care of your wishes for your husband and father. Do you know if he wanted to be buried or if cremation was something he had preferred?" This happened to her often. Jess' mind abruptly flashed to her and Afton in the basement of that funeral home, in the morgue where there was a crematory. Afton's husband and Jess' lover —one in the same— was in a body bag that the two of them had transported there. Sam Drury had threatened them. There was a struggle. He tried to kill his wife, Afton, with his bare hands. And Jess, his mistress, saved Afton's life at the expense of killing Sam from a blow to the head with a fireplace poker. They disposed of his body downstairs in the fires of that crematory. Burned down to basic elements and dried bone fragments, there was no trace left on this earth of Sam Drury. Jess forced herself to focus. That shared secret with Afton was one they would take to their own graves.

Laney woke up with a headache. She had too much wine the night before with her sisters while they shared easy conversation, venting, and much laughter. The three of them listened to and understood each other. Laney didn't feel like Brad could entirely grasp where she was coming from whenever she attempted to speak to him about raising their boys to make good choices now so they could one day grow up to be responsible men. The girl time had recharged Laney, and her frame of mind was positive this morning.

On her way to the kitchen for ibuprofen and a cup of coffee, she could smell pancakes. It was a rush-off-to work and school morning. It wasn't typical for them to cook anything big for breakfast on those days. Brad caught Laney's eye the moment she stepped into the kitchen. She had thrown on a pair of pink pajama bottoms to match the tank top she wore to bed. "Before you ask," Brad said to her, as she spotted the boys both with sleepy eyes and messy hair, shoveling pancakes in their mouths at the kitchen table. A gallon of milk and two tall glasses were on the table between them. "I have a little extra time this morning for cleanup." He was referring to the dishes on the counter and the stovetop that Laney had already noticed. She smiled at him.

"Hi mom," Luke spoke first, and Liam lifted his milk glass in the air at her before he guzzled it down.

"Good morning you two...or three," she added as Brad walked past her with a heaping plate of pancakes and gave her a quick peck on the lips as he did.

"Eat with us," Brad offered.

"Maybe just a small one, but then I have to get ready," she stated, as she walked over to the counter to pour herself a cup of coffee that Brad had already brewed. He was good to her. She knew that. She appreciated what they shared. Life was special with her boys, all three of them. Mornings like this reminded Laney of that.

On Saturday, Laney was about to leave the house for errands when she rummaged through her handbag in search of her car keys. Instead, she found Liam's cell phone. Today was the day he could have it back. She was just going to leave it on the kitchen table, because the boys were both still asleep in their room upstairs. A text came through when Lancy placed the phone down. The name of the neighbor girl, Shey, appeared and Laney read the first few sentences that were visible without opening up the entire message.

A friend wants a starter kit. How much $? I need more mango too. No charge for me, right?

An emoji with a winky face followed those words. First, Laney had no idea what a starter kit even was, or the meaning of mango. She set her son's phone down and reached for her own. Minutes later, she discovered from Google that mango was a JUUL pod flavor, and a starter kit included a JUUL device, a USB charging dock, and four flavors. She also found a $49.99 online price for a starter kit. *So her son was selling these, and refilling orders for flavors? Well, no, the hot little neighbor girl got hers for free. What was she giving her son in return then?* Laney felt sickened by the thought. Liam was underage to be buying these things. And yet he somehow had gotten his hands on it. A part of her wanted to race upstairs and shake her son from his sleep to demand answers. But it was 11 a.m., and she had things to accomplish today. She would confront him later. Now, however, she opened the stainless-steel refrigerator door and grabbed the open bottle of Moscato from the bottom shelf. Only she drank wine. Brad preferred an occasional beer. She twisted off the lid and drank directly from the bottle. There was no time to sip a glass. She only wanted a swallow, just enough to take the edge off. She closed her eyes for a moment. It would be a matter of minutes before her body would absorb not just the alcohol but a feeling of calm that she desperately needed right now. She was brand new at parenting teenagers, but Laney had been a middle school educator long enough to know that her son was on a definite path to becoming one of those kids who couldn't ward off trouble.

Chapter 5

"I noticed you took your phone back today," Laney spoke to Liam as he helped her carry in the grocery bags from her car in the garage. No one else was home. Laney wasn't going to wait for Brad to have this confrontation.

"I did," Liam nodded as he spoke and coughed at the same time. He had been tolerating a dry cough for the last week or so.

"You've stopped vaping, right?" she asked him, as they both started to unpack the bags on the kitchen table and counter.

"I have." Liam was only compliant because he knew that's what his mother wanted to hear. She looked at him. Really looked at her son. He was growing up. The features on his face were changing. Less boy. More man. He looked like Brad. Those dark blue eyes were going to get him far with the ladies. She cringed at the thought. *Ladies? He was still just a boy. Her boy.*

"Can I see your phone for a second?" Laney asked him in a very direct tone, and Liam stopped what he was doing and started at her. Brad was right. Their son, both of their boys, were now taller than her at almost 5-foot-7. *How had they gone so quickly from being little boys to looking like they were on the verge of becoming young men?*

"What? Why?" There was that dry cough again. "You said I could have it back on Saturday. Was I not supposed to take it off the table? I thought you left it there for me?"

Laney nodded. "I did. And I'm not taking it away again. I just want to see it." She was on a mission to read Liam's reply to the earlier message from Shey. Liam reached inside his pocket and it was as if he was in slow motion. It took him forever to hand his phone to his mother. Once he did, he watched her, and he stayed silent. But he knew if she read the text exchange with Shey, his state of being in trouble was about to get far worse.

She tried to contain her reaction. Liam had responded to Shey's message.

Tell your friend $50 cash. And for the mango, a BJ would be awesome.

Laney was 45 years old. She was not worldly or widely experienced with sexual partners. Brad had been her first and only since she was a teenager. She inhaled a slow breath through her nostrils. She was a teenager once too. She was curious and hormonal, and had given in to those temptations. She couldn't lash out at her son over this. She needed to remain calm. Or at least try to.

"Where are you getting the money to buy these JUUL kits that you are reselling?"

Liam knew he couldn't lie to his mother. He paused, or stalled, to cough. But this time the air expelled from his lungs sounded forced. "Online. I used your Amazon account." That account was linked to Laney's email. She knew for certain she never received confirmation purchase emails. He probably had changed the email address to his own for those purchases. From this moment on, her password would be changed, and she would log off that account every single time. She and Brad also needed to pay closer attention to the charges on their credit card statement. That seemed like the easy fix. The difficult, next to impossible task, was going to be getting Liam to stop all of his involvement with vaping. *Both sales and using.*

"You're done sneaking around like that. Do you hear me?" Liam didn't react. He only waited, because he knew his mother was not finished with him. "I want you to go to your room or wherever it is that you are hiding this stash. I want the stuff you are selling and inhaling. All of it." Liam started to walk away. "Wait..." He stopped. "I'm not taking your phone away. You're grounded until... I don't know. But seeing Shey is going to be out of the question for a long time."

"But mom! Please. We are friends. We grew up together for chrissakes!"

"Don't even think about telling me that she's like a sister to you. Sexual favors are hardly sibling-like." Surprisingly, Laney's face did not turn red as she spoke those words aloud. But Liam's did. She watched him look down at the floor. This was the part where she could have screamed at him until her throat felt sore.

"Liam. You're thirteen. Your body may feel ready for those things, but you're not. If you were older, I wouldn't want to know this. I still don't want to know this. It's private. There are boundaries between a mother and son. But damn it, you are a kid. My kid. And I have a responsibility to guide you and help you make the right decisions. No more vaping or selling. You owe me for all of the Amazon purchases that you made on the sly. And as for Shey—"

"Mom please. I know. Stop talking about it."

When Liam took his phone back from his mother, he left the room in silence. *And likely feeling the humiliation.* Laney didn't call him back to help her unpack and put away all of the groceries. In fact, she didn't speak at all. She only felt defeated. It wasn't too long ago when her father took away her last pack of Camels. So she smoked Brad's cigarettes. And sex —once her mother discovered she was doing it— was not something she gave up either, nor had she been able to put those desires on hold until she was a few years older. Not much was going to change, Laney realized that. She left the groceries, and emptied that open bottle of Moscato from the refrigerator when she poured herself a very full glass.

Skye watched the little ones playing at the park as she pushed Bella in a swing. The slide and the swings were the only two forms of recreation that she was interested in experiencing at every park at this stage. There was a boy and girl, probably two and four years old, playing in the sand pit near the swings. Skye observed how protective the big sister was of her little brother.

There was a set of twins, grade-school age, running through the tall grass. Raising Bella had caused many things to surface in her mind and heart. Things that Skye was certain had never occurred to her before.

A young mother, at least a decade younger than Skye, waddled through the park after her toddler, a girl who looked the same age as Bella. She stopped to lift her child into a swing next to where Skye was pushing Bella. She looked every bit of nine months pregnant. Skye groaned to herself. She remembered how miserable she felt carrying Bella. She hated being sick. She didn't want to gain weight. Pregnancy was not pleasant for her, especially at thirty-eight years old. Bella's arrival was worth it though, as Skye knew in her lifetime she would only give birth to one child.

"Hi," the young mother spoke first.

Skye smiled. "How much more time before baby number two arrives?"

"Eight days," the woman sighed and then smiled wide.

"Good for you. You're almost there. I really hated being pregnant. I only wanted the end result," Skye laughed as she referred to Bella, who was swinging back and forth directly in front of her. Her mop of thick, dark hair was blowing with the wind.

"Just one for you?" she asked Skye.

"Yes, just my Bella," Skye smiled, and pushed away the earlier thoughts she had as she watched the siblings playing in the park together.

"I was like you," the woman began, "I only wanted one child. And then I started to get all philosophical about wanting her to have someone to hold her hand all the way through life. Not just me for part of her life, and not her life partner one day. But blood. A sibling. There's really no connection like it." Skye momentarily thought of Afton and Laney. They were close now, and she could not imagine her life without either of them being there for her, and she for them.

"I barely beat the clock having one child, if you know what I mean," Skye stated. "It's just not realistic for me to have more."

"There's always surrogacy," she suggested, and Skye pondered that for a long moment before she responded.

"Yeah... there is, isn't there." Her body would not have to bear the stress of pregnancy, but the end result could still be another child of her own, a sibling for Bella. A sister or brother *to hold her hand all the way through life.* Those words and the prospect of surrogacy stayed with Skye.

Afton's skin was perspiring. Her new haircut swept over her eyes. She was on her knees in the middle of Knox's bed. Correction. Their bed. He was behind her. Plunging inside of her. Thrusting. She called out his name more than once. And she climaxed just as he did, and then they both fell onto the bed naked, beside each other. Knox's chest was rising and falling at a rapid rate. He turned to his side and propped himself up on his elbow. "I can't get enough of you."

She giggled like a schoolgirl. "The desire is mutual." Knox found his way on top of her body, buried his face in her chest, and took a nipple in his mouth. She tightened between her legs again. "How is it possible that I can even walk?" He laughed out loud. They did make love often.

The passion between them began to mount again as Knox kissed his way down her body. Her breasts. Her navel. Between her legs. And then her phone on the nightstand beside their bed rang.

"Oh God," she took Knox's face in her hands near her bent knees. "Sorry love." It was alright. They were both utterly satisfied from the afternoon sex they had already indulged in.

Skye was calling her.

Afton cleared her throat first. "Hi honey," she said, when she answered.

"Hey Aft! Did I catch you a bad time?"

No, just about to have another orgasm, courtesy of this sexy man I am blessed to call mine. Afton smiled at her own thoughts. "Um, no. Knox and I were just. Never mind. What's going on?"

Skye could have read into what Afton didn't finish saying, but she was too focused on what she wanted to talk about. "We just left the park, and we are close to your house. Do you mind if we stop by? There's something on my mind."

"Of course you can come over," Afton glanced at a very naked Knox beside her, and he abruptly jumped up and off the bed to get back into his pants. Afton quickly ended the phone call, and started searching for her own clothes sprawled out all over their bedroom's hardwood flooring.

Knox laughed as they hurried to dress themselves. "Why does this feel so urgent?"

"Well my sister and toddler are minutes away, and I really don't want it to be that obvious to her what we've been doing."

Knox understood. "Can we pick up where we left off later?"

Afton nearly blushed at the thought. "I sure hope so," she winked at him.

"So is little Bella Gallant coming over too?"

"She is," Afton smiled. She relished the thought of seeing her precious niece, but it especially warmed her heart to witness how much Knox enjoyed her. And she him.

Both Afton and Skye watched Knox and Bella through the glass French doors that led outside to a spacious backyard. He lifted her up into his arms to show her the bird feeder at the far end of the property, near the tree line.

"He's really amazing with her, with kids I mean," Skye spoke carefully. She never wanted Afton to read anything into her words. She cared about Knox, but only as the man who made her big sister happy. That's all. She did see how he played the role of an uncle in Bella's life. But really, Knox was the closest thing to a father that Bella had. Skye would never admit that to Afton, but that's how she was beginning to feel. She wanted the two of them to sustain their connection. There really was no such thing as a traditional family anymore. They all cared about each other. That's all that mattered.

"He is," Afton agreed. "Those two are good for each other, you know." Afton's words sort of caught Skye off guard because she believed that, but would never say it out loud as Afton just did.

"I know," Skye spoke in barely a whisper.

"It's okay. I want Bella to grow up knowing what a wonderful person Knox is, and to feel his love."

"I want that, too," Skye smiled. "Thank you, Aft."

Afton saw the tears in her eyes. "What's going on? You're getting all sappy on me." They giggled. But behind the mask of laughter, Afton wondered if Skye had regrets about not involving her baby's biological father in her life.

"I want Bella to have a sibling, a sister or a brother to grow up with. I'm not going to live until the end of time, at least not until the end of Bella's time. I just don't want her to be alone. I don't mean I doubt she will find a partner or friends she will love like family. I mean blood."

"You're serious about this? Skye, have you forgotten how much you loathed the whole process of being pregnant?" And not to mention she was forty years old.

"No. Believe me, I don't want to put my body through that — even if I could get pregnant again."

"So what exactly are you saying?"

"Surrogacy..."

"No way?" Afton thought about that for a moment. "So would you utilize Bella's father again?" She didn't want to directly say the word *use*, even though that's what she believed Skye had initially done.

"I am seriously thinking about it, yes. But no, Bella's father would not be a part of this equation. The baby would be a half sibling to her because, if I can, I want to use my own eggs. I haven't even seen a doctor. I'm only at the stage where I think I really do want this and I need your opinion, your wisdom, your advice. Whatever you can offer me."

With intensity now, Afton watched Knox and Bella. She was chasing him through the grass. Those miniature legs were trying so hard. Her squeals, heard inside too, were the sweetest sound in the world. Knox stopped when one of Bella's little sandals came off. He knelt down to her on the ground and with both of his hands he softly and gracefully helped put that tiny shoe back on her bare foot. Afton froze at the compassion and the love this man had for a child that was not his blood. That wasn't an innovative realization at all. But she did have a brand-new thought that was slowly seeping into her mind right now and attempting to snatch her breath. She could feel her own heart rate quicken.

"You think it's a terrible idea, don't you?" Skye broke her concentration.

"Not at all," Afton was quick to admit, as she turned away from the view outside. "Go see your doctor to get checked out. I would say time is of the essence. If you have healthy eggs, I think you should do this. For Bella. For yourself."

Skye reached for Afton, and they fell into each other's arms. Afton was afraid to admit what she was thinking. *How could something crazy make so much sense?* She didn't want to share this with Skye. Not just yet. There was someone else she had to speak to first.

Chapter 6

Knox studied Afton for a moment. She caught him staring.

"You have something on your mind," he spoke first. She had been distracted ever since her sister left.

"I do," Afton admitted.

"Does it have to do with Skye or Bella?"

"It does actually. Can we talk?" she asked and reached for his hand. They left the kitchen and walked into the living room to sit down in the middle of the ivory leather sectional together. Knox didn't want to speculate that Afton had bad news to share with him, but the way she was acting confused him. It was almost as if she was hesitant to tell him something or ask something of him. He waited for her to speak.

"There's a part of me that's you now. You have touched my life, my soul, in a way that no one else ever has. I have a place tucked inside my heart where only you have been. I know you love me," she paused, "I feel how special I am to you. My heart is full, Knox." He took her hand and gently brought two of her fingers to his lips. She continued speaking her mind, emptying her soul with every spoken word. "I wonder about a place in your heart. Not the one for me, or any loves prior to me. I'm referring to the place that's vacant, that's reserved for a child. Your own child." Knox didn't want to have this conversation. That was a sealed vault. He convinced himself that dream had died. He could live with that truth. As long as he had Afton. She was worth any sacrifice to him. He loved her endlessly. And it almost angered him now to know she wanted to open that wound for him. "Knox... having a child of your own will take *you* to a place you've never been. I see how you are with Bella. I know how much you ache to be a father."

"I love that little one. And I love you. Love in those ways are enough for me. I promise you."

"I know you believe that, but what if you had the chance to be a father?"

"Afton, we know that's not possible." She was fifty years old, and there was no way she could ever be the mother of his child. They both knew that. Knox, however, had been through rigorous fertility tests and never received a negative result. His ex-wife had been the one unable to get pregnant, no matter what methods they resorted to. But it was possible for him to biologically father a child.

Afton could not give Knox that gift herself, but she could give her blessing for him to father the second child that Skye wanted to have. *But could she truly handle that? Could she step back and literally watch the love of her life and her baby sister share a child? They could co-parent a child. Back and forth. And together at times. But what if that act alone brought the two of them together as a couple? After all, they had been attracted to each other once.* That was a risk and the mere thought of it broke Afton's heart. But she had to be confident in Knox's love for her. That was what brought her to this revelation. This wasn't about the two of them. This had everything to do with the prospect of a child for Knox to have of his very own.

All Afton had to do was speak the words to him. It was the first stride in order to make this a reality.

"What if you fathered a child via surrogate?"

"I'm not sure where you are going with this. We both have our careers. You've already raised your children and will soon begin enjoying that next phase of your life as a grandmother. A hot and sexy one, I might add." She grinned at him, and allowed him to continue. "I'm not sure that a baby is what we need. I love our life together, Afton. It's just beginning. Let's grow old together. Just the two of us."

"The idea of a surrogate is strange, I know," Afton stated. "Nothing is for certain, and you are the only person I have told this to, but my heart is in this not just for you but for my sister." Knox creased his brow.

"Skye? What does any of this have to do with Skye?"

"She wants another baby... but she doesn't want to carry it. She's considering a surrogate."

Knox's face lost its color. He shook his head a few times. "You can't be serious! She asked you to let me father her child? Haven't we already risked losing you in both of our lives?" This was the first time in a very long time that Knox had brought up his and Skye's one-night stand.

"No. Absolutely not. Skye has no idea. She's focused on doing this on her own, and likely through a donor this time. I don't even know what she's thinking."

"Then this would upset her if she knew what you were suggesting of us."

"Does it upset you?"

"Yes," Knox admitted. "Yes, because we hurt you in the worst way. Unintentionally, yes, but you were broken nonetheless. Why would you want us to do something that could bond us like that?"

Because she loved them both that much. And unconditionally. "I recognize what Skye needs to give Bella, for her childhood and her future. And I also see this as something I could give you." She clearly meant in an indirect way.

"You're not saying that you think Skye and I should raise a baby together and *be together?*"

Afton smiled softly at him. "No. I'm not that selfless. I am keeping you for as long as you will have me."

"Afton," Knox paused, because his mind was reeling and he wasn't even sure how he was going to put into words what he was about to say. "I consider myself an all or nothing kind of man. I don't see how I could ever be a part-time dad."

That never occurred to her. But Knox had a valid point. Maybe her idea was more absurd than she initially thought. But she did have one more thing to say to him. "I understand," Afton began, "but just consider how life doesn't always ask of us to do something the right way, or in the expected manner. Sometimes, we just have to take what we can get, reap those rewards, and make it enough. Look at it as getting something instead of nothing."

Knox was speechless for a long time. Afton wished she was able to read his thoughts, but she couldn't, and now she feared she had made a mistake by suggesting they change their lives in such a drastic way. They were so happy. *Why curse that?*

"I need some time to think," Knox stated, honestly. "This is overwhelming. What I really wish I could bring myself to say right now is no. No I do not want to do this. I love us as we are. Can't we just stay this way? I wish I could say all of that and mean it entirely. But... you really are making me think. Afton, we have to be sure, as a unit, that this is the right choice for us. And what about Skye? She could throw this back in our faces and tell us both to fuck off."

Afton giggled. "She may do just that, at first. But she'll come around. Just as I can see you are doing."

Knox pulled her close to him, almost with a forceful eagerness. He kissed her long and hard. And when they pulled apart from each other, she saw the tears in his eyes. He wanted this for himself, and Afton wished to be the one to lead him to it.

He kissed her again and with more intensity. Neither one of them wanted to talk anymore. Not about a subject that could change their lives quickly and for the rest of forever. They only yearned to hold onto what was certain right now. That was each other. Their love. And passion that enabled them to shut out the rest of the world.

Chapter 7

Skye's career as a website designer allowed her the luxury of working from home, while Bella attended a private daycare and preschool full-time. Skye was home alone, working, and it was mid-morning when she was interrupted by the doorbell. She wasn't expecting anyone, but she got up from her desk in her office and walked through her house to answer the door.

"Afton? Hi. What's going on? Did I miss a text or a call?"

"No. It's just me showing up the old-fashioned way. Odd huh?" Afton had been a professional photographer in Saint Paul for almost thirty years. Her schedule was flexible, and because she couldn't concentrate on anything else but having this conversation with Skye, here she was.

"You can stop by unannounced anytime. It's your new living quarters where we all know we need to forewarn you that we are popping in."

Afton closed the front door behind her. She frowned. "What? Why?"

"Like I didn't notice how flushed your cheeks were last time. A nooner with Knox, perhaps?" Skye laughed out loud, and Afton tried not to look as embarrassed as she felt.

"Stop it. But really, it feels like a dream, you know?"

"Who would have believed half the things that have happened in our family? I'm sure mom is shaking her head at us from beyond."

"We're doing okay," Afton reassured her, but she knew what Skye meant. And she wasn't even aware of how Afton was an accomplice in covering up her own husband's demise. That was going to remain her shared secret with Jess Robertson. *Forever.*

They walked into the kitchen together. "Can I get you something?" It was too early for alcohol.

"No. I just need you to hear me. I have something on my mind that I want to share with you. Just listen, okay?" Afton repeated herself because that's all she really wanted from Skye at this point. Just for her to listen and be open-minded. She and Knox had not discussed it again. And now Afton knew it was going to be up to Skye if this was going to become a reality for all of them.

"Well now you're worrying me. Out with it. Just tell me." Skye had absolutely no idea how Afton was about to change her life.

"Have you made a doctor's appointment yet?"

"No, but it's on my to-do list for this week."

"Are you still feeling all-in about giving Bella a sibling via surrogate?" Afton made no reference to the likelihood of using a sperm donor.

"Yeah... I mean, I don't think about it day and night, but I do want this for Bella. I also know it would be wonderful to raise her and a baby close together in age. Mom spaced us girls out every five years and let's be honest, you and I didn't have a chance to bond growing up." Skye sure did appreciate both of her older sisters as constants in her life now though.

"Maybe you should sit down?" Afton now felt nervous about this.

"I don't want to."

"Okay fine." *Here goes nothing. No, it was something. And it had the potential to be something special for everyone.* "It's about Knox."

"Oh thank God!" Skye reacted, because that's what she did. "I was beginning to think this was something that I did."

"Well it's also about you. You and Knox."

Skye refrained from reacting this time. *Hadn't they put that behind them?*

"Not that," Afton responded, reading her mind. "I love him more every single day. He completes me. I feel like he has given me everything I need. I want to do the same for him." Skye listened raptly. "He's almost seven years younger than me. There's still time in his life for him to be a father. I've raised my children and I am preparing for my first grandbaby. But Knox deserves to still experience fatherhood."

"Afton, don't. Don't leave him and send him off to find a younger, fertile woman. He will never adore anyone else the way he does you. Stop trying to be a martyr here. Just love him and live out all of your years together."

"I'm not leaving him. As I told him, I'm not that selfless. I want what I want, and that's Knox. Forever. But I do want him to be a father. I've thought at length about what you mentioned... regarding having a surrogate carry a baby."

"But the baby wouldn't be yours. Just Knox's? And are you prepared to start all over raising a child? You said so yourself, that part of your life is done and over."

"I would want Knox to raise his baby with the mother of his child. They could co-parent. I could be like a step-mother." *Or an aunt again, as she already was.*

"Wait. Wouldn't the mother be a donor? Those women have no rights, nor do they want them. You're not understanding how this works, Aft."

"She would definitely be the baby's mother. *You* could be the baby's mother, Skye."

Skye stood still. She didn't want to move. She couldn't. She never spoke either. What Afton suggested to her didn't make any damn sense. She moved unsteadily toward one of the closest kitchen chairs. Afton only watched her and waited for her to respond. This, she knew, was a shock.

"Have you lost your mind? Why would you put Knox and me together like that? I mean, after what happened, and how you were able to overcome it. It's just wrong. I can't even fathom what in the hell you are thinking."

"Knox had the very same reaction."

"What? Christ! You told him this?"

"I told him that Bella could be getting a sibling because you want that for her. I also told him how you likely would have a donor, which is completely your private business, but that you want to use a surrogate for the pregnancy. Think about the prospect of Knox finally becoming a father, and for you to have an involved parent in your child's life. It seems too easy."

"Easy? Would it be easy for you to live knowing the love of your life and your sister share a child? It's not fair that you would ask that of either of us. It's wrong. And it would be destructive to our relationship and probably eventually to yours with Knox. Use your head, consider how a child would forever connect him to me. Haven't we just spent the last several months putting something that happened one night behind us? We've healed. Just leave it be now."

"Knox was angry too. He's still confused and apprehensive, and probably more in agreement with you than you know. But I really believe, at the end of the day, he's a little hopeful too. Look how wonderful he is with Bella. Why would you both want to just grab a donor when you could create a life, in a lab of course, knowing your baby will have two, loving and supportive parents."

"No. Absolutely not. I would never do that to you. End of story, Afton. Go home."

"I'm not leaving."

"You are fucking crazy."

"And you, deep down, know that as absurd as it sounds... it could be the answer for everyone."

"Don't. You'll end up hating me for taking a huge part of Knox away from you. This absurd idea of yours would disrupt the happy life that you've finally been able to create. Nothing is standing in the way of the two of you now. Sam is gone. Your kids are grown. Have sex in the middle of the day. Go away on an adventure because you can. Love him because you deserve him."

"I will do all of those things, and together we will be blissfully happy. But I'll always know deep in my soul that Knox is incomplete. He yearns for a child. It's been his greatest dream. I need to give that to him, and I want you, someone I also love so deeply, to help me do that. In turn, you can give your baby what Bella doesn't have. A daddy."

"I can't talk about this anymore."

"I'll go."

But before she left, Afton looked back, and said, "Make a doctor's appointment. At least get checked out." When Afton closed the door behind her, a small part of Skye wished for it to no longer be possible for her to be the biological mother of another child. While that truth would crush her for Bella's sake, it would also ultimately safeguard her relationship with her sister.

Chapter 8

Laney had just gotten home. She left as soon as the school day ended, and she was by herself. Luke had baseball practice, and Liam was at a student council meeting. She was relieved he was doing something productive, but nonetheless he had recently grunted that he was not going to run again, or be a part of anything extracurricular in the eighth grade.

There was time to start dinner and throw a load of laundry in the washer before Brad and the boys would be home. She changed into a pair of athletic shorts and her favorite sleeveless white t-shirt. And while she decided on grilling chicken for dinner, she poured herself a glass of Moscato.

She prepared to light the grill on the deck outside, but the doorbell rang just as Laney stepped out the patio door. She wasn't expecting anyone, but she backtracked her steps into the house to answer the door.

Skye was standing on Laney's front porch.

"Well hi there," was all Laney was able to speak before Skye interrupted in her typical hurry-up-and-say-it fashion.

"You have to talk some sense into Afton!" Skye brushed past her older sister by five years, and stood in the foyer.

Laney could not see the need to do that. But it did happen once before. "Now the last time you implied that Afton needed redirection, she was having an affair with a younger man. I can't imagine what could be wrong now." Laney saw the look on Skye's face, and immediately she knew this matter had to be serious. "Wait. This doesn't have anything to do with you again, does it?"

"Only because Afton is making this about me! Damn it. You're not going to believe this one. I respect that our sister's life began again at fifty, but this is too much for me. And it's going to slowly chip away at, and then destroy our family."

"You need to calm down. Let's sit. Can I get you a drink?" Laney certainly needed her full glass in the kitchen.

"No. I want a clear head for this."

"I'm listening," Laney told her as they walked into her kitchen together and the first thing Skye watched her do was take a generous sip of alcohol.

"You know that I have been considering a surrogate for another baby." Laney smiled at the thought. She liked the idea of Skye giving Bella a sibling. "Afton thinks she has a genius idea. She doesn't want me to use a sperm donor. She wants to give my baby a real father, one who will love and help raise her, or him. Her proposition would also give Knox the chance to be a father..."

Laney's eyes widened just as she was about to tip her wine glass again. She stopped. She stood straighter. "I don't think I understand what you're saying. Please tell me Afton isn't pushing the two of you together for reasons I can't even comprehend right now!"

"No," Skye had questioned that as well. "It's not like that. She wants Knox. They will be together, but he will be a co-parent with me to our child."

"What kind of soap opera are we living here?" Laney proclaimed. "I can't. I seriously can't believe she would ever think something like that could work."

"Thank you. I told her the exact same thing, practically word for word. Well, I may have thrown in a few prominent curse words too."

"Of course you did," Laney began. "I hope you also told her to never bring up something so ridiculous ever again, and that your life is your own and you will not be intertwining it so intimately with Knox. Again..."

Skye bit her lip and refrained from attempting to defend herself, because that's not what this was about. "For your information, the conception idea would take place in a lab — not the way you are thinking."

Laney watched Skye. Something suddenly changed with her body language. "A part of you wants to consider this. I'm right, aren't I? You have regrets about Bella being fatherless. Knox is wonderful with her, so just imagine him with his own child. Skye, our sister has not thought this completely through. She's blinded by the newness of being in love and wanting to give her man absolutely anything that will make him happy. She isn't even reasoning the craziness of passing a baby back and forth between two homes. You and Knox will be connected with the milestones, the worry-phases, and just the shared joy of it all. I can't imagine Afton being able to stand back and take that. I know I couldn't do it!"

"What I want is for Afton to stop thinking this will work and pushing for it to happen. And I especially wish she had not told Knox. Apparently, he was initially upset and adamantly against it... but then Afton said he seemed a little hopeful. Presumably about his lost chance to have a child of his own."

"Then let them get a surrogate. Keep yourself out of this, Skye." Laney finished the wine in her glass, and went to the refrigerator for the open bottle.

"Am I driving you to drink?" Skye stated and suppressed a giggle.

"Everyone and everything is these days," Laney sighed, and Skye stayed silent. She should not have brought it up. Not even in a joking manner. *So what if Laney enjoyed alcohol?*

Chapter 9

After dinner, Laney was still drinking. The boys appeared oblivious to it, but Brad pulled her aside once they left the kitchen. "Hey, how much have you had to drink tonight?"

Laney turned around to face him. She was very buzzed. She was in that fog of intoxication. That state of having impaired senses, and not giving a damn. She was worried about her sisters. She wanted to keep their family close. She started drinking more after Skye left, and then when her sons came home she tried to hide how off balance and tipsy she truly felt.

"Just a few glasses," she answered, placing her open palms on her husband's chest.

"A few too many," Brad spoke, attempting to make eye contact with his wife, but hers was fleeting.

"Why don't we sneak upstairs and lock the door," she tried to come on to him. Brad took her hands in his and removed them from touching him.

"Stop. The boys are here, and if you weren't drunk you would be the one telling me we have to wait."

She laughed out loud. "Riiight..." She hiccupped as she spoke, and Brad was disgusted with her behavior.

"No more wine. I am going to throw that shit out. Just quit cold turkey. Stop thinking you need it to function. Yes, we are raising teenagers, but so is every other person in America. We will survive. Sober up!"

"Fuck you..." Laney kept her voice low, but Brad heard her.

"This isn't you. Go upstairs and take a shower. And then just go to bed. I'll take care of things down here."

Laney felt the tears well up in her eyes. She had never seen disappointment like that from him. She only left the room and did what he suggested because she was afraid she might break down in front of him. Her drunken state gave her very little control over her emotions. Brad was right. She needed to stop turning to a glass of wine to ease her mind over everything that came up in their lives.

She stood in the steam from the shower for the longest time. She already felt better. She had a towel on her head and another towel wrapped around her body. When she opened the bathroom door, Brad was waiting for her with two ibuprofen and a glass of iced water. "Take these to keep a headache away in the morning." She smiled at him. He always did know what she needed.

"Thank you." She put the pills in her mouth, one at a time, and tipped back swallows of water. "Brad..." she caught her husband's attention. "I'm sorry." he nodded. "You're right. I need to stop, or slow down, or something. Skye stopped by. She and Afton are at odds. She asked me to help her... and I don't know if this is something I can fix."

"You can tell me what it is, and maybe I can help," Brad was seated on the side of their bed. He wore a pair of gray gym shorts and a red t-shirt and he was barefoot. He was boyish and masculine at the very same time. She was attracted to him. Always.

Laney stood in the middle of their bedroom, still holding the glass of water he gave her. She knew she should finish it. It would hydrate her and counteract some of the alcohol she drank in excess tonight. "Skye wants to use her eggs, a donor, and a surrogate to have another baby." Brad didn't think that was any surprise, or such a terrible thing. "But Afton strongly believes her baby needs a father, active and loving in its life. We all see that Bella is missing out on that. Afton also wants to give Knox his lost chance to father a child."

"You're kidding me! She wants them to be together?"

"Not in that sense. Conception will happen in a lab, and co-parenting will be the plan after the baby is born."

Brad shook his head. "That's not normal thinking. It will never work. Afton will feel left out, and Knox will be torn between his child and the woman he loves."

"I don't know what's going to happen. I need to talk to Afton, but the more I thought about it tonight, the more I got lost in drinking. I'm sorry, babe. Please don't be ashamed of me." Brad saw the tears in her eyes, and nothing crushed him more than to see her cry.

She stepped toward him in only her towel. She stood directly in front of him. "I'm not ashamed of you. Just worried about you. I'm relieved that you see what I'm saying. No more drinking, Lane."

To move forward from this subject, Laney removed the towel from her head and she let her wet hair fall loose. She knew that turned him on. His eyes widened, as he watched her. "You need to get some rest."

"Not yet," she whispered. "Where are the boys?"

"Outside shooting hoops. I told them you have a headache and need to rest, so they won't be coming in here to say goodnight."

"Sounds like you have something more in mind for me than rest," Laney teased him. He put his hands on her waist, and she wiggled out of her towel.

She stood naked in front of him. He touched her round breasts. She closed her eyes. He met his mouth with her nipples, one and then the other. She tightened between her legs. He found her core with his fingers. She whimpered. He touched her slowly, but consistently. Her hands were gripping his shoulders while he sat still in front of her on their bed. He touched her tenderly and repeatedly. She was close. Her legs were shaky. Her grip tightened on the back of his shoulders. Two of his fingers slipped inside her while he thumbed her most sensitive spot. She wanted this. She needed him to take her over the edge. Sex was their sanctuary. Nothing else mattered when it was just the two of them. Doing this.

Her breathing was rapid, she called out his name, biting her bottom lip and purposely trying to keep her voice down even though the boys were outside. Her release had driven him to the edge as well. He ripped off his shirt. She pulled off his shorts and underwear. She crawled on top of him on their bed and he kissed her full and hard on the mouth. Even though she had brushed her teeth, Brad could still taste the alcohol. He pushed that thought aside as his wife straddled him. She eagerly helped him inside her. She rocked over him. Her head started to hurt, but she ignored that. He was far inside her when they found their rhythm together. She pounced. He met her every move with every inch of himself. He touched her core again, repeatedly, as their rhythm finally brought them to that shared place of passion and ecstasy.

She laid beside her husband while he slept. Her boys had long been back inside the house, showered, and went to bed. Laney then made her way into the kitchen. She told herself no. She tried to focus on Brad's words. *Throw it out. Just quit. Stop thinking that you need it.*

She twisted off the cap of the wine bottle. She stood over the sink with the intention of pouring it out. Every drop of it. Instead, she held tightly to the neck of that bottle. Her hand trembled as she brought the open bottle to her mouth and wet her lips with it. She gave in and drank. She tipped the bottle back again, and some of the wine splashed out and onto the floor. She drank harder and faster until her eyes burned. But she didn't care. She needed to empty that bottle. In the middle of the night when no one was watching. Once she did it, she would be done. *No more*, Laney told herself.

Chapter 10

Knox felt sneaky, as if this was a betrayal somehow. Instead of going directly home after he left the hospital, he drove to Skye's house.

He slowed his pace as he walked up the driveway. He contemplated turning around, getting back in his car and driving away from there. But this, what Afton believed they could do —or should do because it made ideal sense for everyone— was weighing so heavily on his mind. And now, being here, was his way of admitting that he was either open to the idea, or looking for closure. He had to know if Skye was completely against bringing a child into this world, one that would be his.

When Knox and Afton spoke about her conversation with Skye, she told him it had not gone well. But then she mentioned that Skye was prone to changing her mind after thinking things through.

Skye saw him outside through the front windows of her house. She was about to leave to pick up Bella from daycare. Knox was alone. He had been to her home with Afton so it wasn't as if this was the first time he was back there since the night they got together, when neither of them knew their connection to Afton. *And besides, they were past that!*

He seemed hesitant to walk up to her porch. Skye opened her front door and hung her body halfway out. "Hey, are you lost?" she laughed loudly when he turned back around. It appeared that he was going to leave without ever letting his presence known.

Knox chuckled, shook his head, and looked down at the ground before he answered her. "Lost in thought about what I can do to make this feel less awkward."

She rolled her eyes. "Get over yourself, Manning. You love my sister, so there is no possible way we can share a child." Leave it to Skye to speak her mind to ease everyone else's. "I have a few minutes before picking up Bella, why don't you come in?"

"If you have to go, this can wait. I was just on my way home from the hospital and—"

"You're here. Let's just talk about it." *And put it to rest.*

Knox stepped inside. He purposely stayed in the immense foyer. He didn't want to go in the living room alone with her. She sensed as much, so she stood there with him.

"Should I go first, or do you have something that you would like to say?" *Knox, the gentleman.* Skye smiled. *What woman in her right mind would not want this beautiful man to father her child?*

Even if the proposed plan was through artificial insemination and a surrogate. Snagging those genes alone were awfully tempting.

"I always have something to say," she giggled. *That she did.* Knox chuckled under his breath. "You're here because you either want my help with squashing Afton's ridiculous idea, or you need to talk about the possibility of it actually becoming a reality."

"Both, actually," Knox had his hands in the deep side pockets of his navy dress pants. "We both shut her down the moment Afton spoke of it. We instantly wanted to put Afton first, to protect her from being hurt by the two of us again." Skye wholeheartedly agreed, but kept quiet to hear him out. "And then, for me, it started to settle in my soul. There suddenly was this lingering possibility that I could have a child of my own to love and to raise, and still have Afton by my side. For me, that would be the best of both worlds. But how fair would that be for you? And especially for Afton in the long run. Could she handle us sharing a co-parenting bond like that? I don't think I could if the situation were reversed. As I said, I won't hurt her. I love her too much."

Skye smiled sincerely at him. "You are a godsend to my sister. I am so grateful she has you. You have made her happier than she's ever been in her entire life, and now she wants to make your greatest wish come true. Afton is trying to give us both this incredible gift, and we can't accept it. I do want to bring a second child into this world for me and Bella. That hasn't changed. I just know I can't lure you into this equation." She never had to share Bella with anyone, and it would be the same for another baby. *Maybe she liked it that way. Fatherless or not, her children would be happy and fulfilled.* Skye refrained from saying that if she was able to choose any father for her child, it would be Knox. No second guessing needed.

"I understand," Knox spoke as if he was going to abruptly end this conversation and leave. He had his answer. Skye was not open to discussing the idea of co-parenting a child with him. There were no pros and cons to rehash or consider. "For what it's worth though, I wanted to be a part of that equation. I think you are a wonderful mother. I also already feel so much a part of the Gallant family." Knox truly loved Bella as his own. And now he could only imagine what giving her a baby brother or sister would be like, if he were the father.

Skye stared at him. She was not expecting what he just said. Perhaps Knox did stop by with hope in his heart for Skye to want him to be her baby's father. And now she would send him away crushed and disappointed. But that's the way it had to be.

Skye was just a few blocks away from the daycare when her phone rang. It was her gynecologist's office calling. She answered while she drove.

"Am I speaking with Skye Gallant?"

"Yes you are."

"I'm calling about your lab results. Dr. Peters would like to see you as soon as your schedule allows."

So her eggs were all dried up. That certainly would make this whole saga a lot less dramatic. She was too old to be a biological mother again.

"I assume this is about my reproductive organs?" Skye asked into the phone.

"Actually, it's regarding your blood work. There are some abnormalities that the doctor would like to address with you."

Abnormalities? So she was low on iron or B12 deficient? Nothing a vitamin couldn't fix.

"I can be there tomorrow."

"Morning or afternoon?"

"Morning."

"Okay, 10 a.m."

"I've got it down."

Skye brushed away any unnecessary worry. And she still held out some hope that not all of her eggs had died off.

Chapter 11

At Afton Photography, located in downtown Saint Paul, there was a makeshift brick wall, painted off-white with gray grout, where Afton took some of her indoor shots. Those two walls met at a corner where Jess Robertson stood in heels, poised against that backdrop. Her dark hair was long with loose curls again. She contemplated wearing it up, for a fitting business-like style, but this was how she wanted people to see her. Casual and approachable. Like one of them.

Afton agreed. Soft. Sincere. Yet professional. That was the look she was going for today for the photographs needed for business cards and advertisement. Already, Robertson Funeral Home, Inc. wanted to introduce Jess as the upcoming mortician and funeral director at Saint Paul's location. She had been working so much with the public that knowing she was still earning her degree had almost been forgotten.

She wore skinny black pants with a modest V-neck blue blouse that accented her eyes. "Smile like you want customers to know you are there for them, but not too cheery because of the unfortunate circumstances," Afton directed her from behind the lens. "Perfect. You're a beauty, Jess." Afton and Jess had a friendship like no other now. They didn't just share a shocking secret that would forever bond them, they were involved in each other's lives more than ever before. While she had been snapping photos, Afton spoke of her youngest sister's choice to have another baby via a surrogate. And then she shared her idea involving Knox.

"Tell me that it is not happening!" Jess hopped off the stool that Afton now had her positioned on.

"It's not happening. Both Skye and Knox adamantly declined in an effort to protect me, which is silly because it was my idea to begin with."

"An idea that makes you seem certifiable." Jess was not kidding.

"Oh shut the hell up."

"No you shut up before you ruin the most amazing thing your life has seen in a very long time. I mean really, who doesn't lay awake at night and fantasize about a hottie like Knox Manning showing up on their doorstep?"

Afton suppressed a giggle. "You're lonely. How long has it been since you've had a man in your bed?"

Jess sighed. "I don't date. I don't have time with school and the apprenticeship at the funeral home."

"As Skye would say, a woman doesn't have to date to have sex."

"True."

"You're still feeling guilty about Sam," Afton noted.

"Sam and Mark. And the way I messed up my life pretty badly."

"It's not a mess, and it certainly wasn't all you. You unexpectedly lost your husband, you're not to blame for that. But then you did kill your lover to save me." Afton laughed, and Jess flipped her off. "But look how you've pulled yourself together. You're on a healthy, successful path. I have no doubt there is a man out there for you, when you're ready. Look around you, they are practically lined up and waiting." *A beautiful, smart, spontaneous, available woman.*

"I know I'm not ready for a relationship, but if I lost ahold of my self-control, I could be at least having sex."

"Do I want to know about this?" Afton asked her.

"You already know Mark's cousin, Patrick, and how I'm working under his direction."

"Stop right there. He's married with small children. I no longer like this idea of you doing anything *under* him."

This time Jess laughed. "Yes I know. I won't repeat a mistake like that again. But you know quite a bit about the temptation of a younger, desirable, man."

"My situation was altogether different. Knox was divorced and I didn't have much of a marriage left."

"You're happy now... which is all that matters."

"I am happy. Unbelievably so."

"Then forget the idea of having Knox father your sister's baby."

"If anyone overheard that..." Afton began, but stopped herself to laugh out loud.

"Right. Most of our conversations should not be intercepted by anyone or anything with ears."

Afton agreed. But they needed to change the subject, as the front door entrance to her studio chimed and she had a customer.

Dr. Linda Peters was a small-framed, stocky woman. She was the obstetrician who delivered Bella, and she had been Skye's gynecologist since she was fifteen years old when her mother thought *it was time she was put on the pill.*

Skye smiled at the woman whose dream career was to deliver babies. She only hoped Dr. Peters could help her to have just one more. Skye planned to ask her personally what she knew about surrogacy and if she could give her some direction. But first, she needed to know if her reproductive eggs were healthy and usable.

"So, Dr. Peters, just tell me outright, do I have a chance to be a biological mother again?"

Dr. Peters smiled softly. "Your eggs are healthy. You actually have a lower percentage of abnormal eggs than most women who are in their forties."

"So there's no reason why we can't go ahead and fertilize one of those healthy eggs?" Skye was elated. She was going to be a mother again. Bella would have a sibling.

Dr. Peters wore a concerned look on her face. "There could be a reason to slow this down." Skye creased her brow. "Your CBC blood work, which reveals your complete blood count, showed some abnormalities in your blood cells. There are common blood disorders like anemia or hemophilia. Then there are more serious blood disorders that can be detected. You have a high level of protein in your blood, and your urine test revealed a significant elevation in protein as well. I would like to refer you to a hematologist-oncologist for further testing."

Skye slowly took in everything her doctor said. She was an intelligent woman, but she only partly comprehended what she was being told. "Okay, I don't know what a hematologist specializes in, but your mention of an oncologist is alarming to me because my first thought was cancer. Is that what you're telling me? I have cancer?"

"One specific test on your blood, a serum protein electrophoresis, measures the amount of abnormal antibodies in the blood. That test result will be read by a specialist. You could have a form of blood cancer, called myeloma."

Skye shook her head. "No, I don't. I feel completely fine. People who have cancer have symptoms and are sick. I am healthy and so are my eggs, you said so yourself. Too much protein in my body doesn't sound all that alarming. I can make dietary changes to correct that, right?"

"Skye," Dr. Peters' voice was calm and nurturing. Like her mother's once upon a time. "Sometimes there are no signs or symptoms. There could be fatigue, frequent infections, loss of appetite or weight loss. Or other things like bone problems, mental fogginess or confusion. Not everyone experiences those."

"What is myeloma? I know you said it's a blood cancer, but define it to me."

"It's a rare, incurable blood cancer of the plasma cells." Skye held her breath. "A plasma cell is a type of white blood cell which originates in the bone marrow. Plasma cells produce antibodies that help fight infection." Skye was only hearing words at this point. She stopped listening once she heard, *incurable*. "Cancerous plasma cells are known as multiple myeloma cells. They create abnormal antibodies, called M proteins, which offer no benefit to the body. As multiple myeloma cells multiply, they crowd out normal plasma cells."

"If it's true... how do I fight this? I have a two-year-old to raise. Have I told you that I am a single parent? I'm only forty years old. There's a lifetime ahead of me still." Skye was rambling with tears welling up in her eyes. Dr. Peters touched her hand.

"I know. Keep those positive thoughts and your strong-willed mindset. It will do you serious good."

"Will it save my life?" Skye felt angry at this unfair news. *She didn't feel sick!*

"It's possible to be in remission to decrease the signs and symptoms. Unfortunately, this disease is known to return in nearly all patients. It's often characterized by recurring cycles of relapse and remission."

"So I could either die, or have limited years of battling a rare form of blood cancer." Skye waited for her doctor to respond. But she didn't. She, of course, did not have those answers for Skye or anyone else. "I sort of feel like I'm being punished here."

"Don't," Dr. Peters spoke. "This is unexpected, I know, but do not blame yourself or wallow in it. You're a strong, independent, and fierce woman. More testing will show us exactly what you're dealing with. Educate yourself on this. A close friend of mine is the specialist I am going to refer you to. He's going to stay one step ahead of this cancer, right along with you."

"Well I need him to be a miracle-worker."

"His name is Dr. Dylan Fruend. His clinic is here on the grounds of Regional Minneapolis. I'll get you his contact information today. As I said, he's a trusted friend, and a phenomenal doctor."

Skye believed she could use someone extraordinary in her life at this awful moment when she felt entirely alone, and hopeless.

Chapter 12

She was in a fog. An appointment in three days with a hematologist oncologist was the only plan Skye had. *Was it a plan of action to conquer the deadliness that was flowing through her veins? Or, would Skye just buy herself some time?* Typically, she planned ahead for everything in her life. It felt strange and terribly disappointing to know she may be forced to start thinking in terms of living one day at a time. If she had this rare form of blood cancer.

It was getting closer to the time she was supposed to pick up Bella at daycare. She couldn't do it though. She texted both Laney and Afton in a group message.

Are either of you free to pick up Bella at daycare at 4:30?

Afton's reply came first.

I'll speak for Laney. She can't. It's 8th grade graduation tonight for her students. I am about to do a photo shoot. Call Knox. He's available and would be happy to help you out. I mean that. Call him.

Skye didn't think about her offer too long. She trusted Knox. She would ask him.

I will do that. Thanks Aft.

Sure. Anytime. Where are you by the way?

Just tied up with something. More like utterly consumed with the shocking and ugly truth that she was likely sick and branded with a short lifespan.

Skye called Knox. He answered on the second ring.

"Hey, are you busy?"

"Not really. I had surgeries all morning and just got home. Afton is doing a photo shoot so I'm basically free until she and I have a late dinner. Need something?"

"Actually, yeah. I just asked Afton and Laney if either of them could pick up Bella from daycare at 4:30. Afton nominated you."

"She did? Well good, because I was just about to offer. May I?"

"Please," Skye spoke. "And thank you. I will call the daycare to let them know you're coming."

"Anything else I should know?" Knox asked.

"No. Um. She eats anything. She loves to play, but you already have that down. I won't be late. You can still plan that dinner with Afton."

"Don't worry about us. Is everything good on your end?"

Skye paused. She couldn't answer that. Not truthfully, and certainly not with a lie. "I have to go, Knox. Thanks again."

She walked the path through Mears Park. Yes, she could have picked up Bella at daycare, but she wasn't ready. Skye needed to think, and to prepare herself to look at her daughter through different eyes. She now could be forced to appreciate every time-ticking moment left with her. And to, eventually, accept that there would be milestones and moments ahead in her daughter's life that she would not be around to share and to celebrate with her. Sure, Skye still had to go through numerous tests and have a plan of action for precisely what she was dealing with. That would certainly make a difference and matter. But what concerned her most right now was making a plan for her daughter's life. *Who would take care of her, and continue to raise her?* And, it was equally as important for Skye to leave behind a sibling for Bella. Now more than ever.

It was a lot to ask, but Skye had carefully thought this through. And it was what she wanted.

She parked her jeep on the driveway on Holly Avenue.

She didn't knock when she made it to the front door. She just turned the door handle and walked in. Her child was in there. She had a right to just barge in without notice. Not that Knox or Afton would mind. Nothing could take away their smiles these days. *How could two people be so damn happy together? Well they should relish every last second…because life was fleeting. And nothing was for keeps or for certain.*

"Hi honey, come on in!" Afton raised her voice from the kitchen. Skye could hear giggles coming from in there, too.

She rounded the corner of that old Victorian house, and saw Bella sitting on a booster seat on a chair at the head of the table. Like a tiny queen. She held a spoon and mastered keeping the macaroni and cheese noodles on it as she scooped it to her mouth.

"Mommy!" Her eyes widened and she, for real, had a cheesy smile.

Her baby girl. "Look at you. Uncle Knox and Aunt Afton sure know how to spoil you." Afton beamed at Skye's reference to Knox. He did, too, actually.

"I want a movie!" Bella blurted out, pushing away her food.

"We did promise she could watch anything of her choice on Netflix after dinner," Knox explained, as he used a napkin to clean her tiny hands and mouth. Skye watched him with her daughter. He was so attentive to her needs. And loving.

"Oh no. We should go home. You and Afton still need to enjoy a nice dinner," Skye attempted to argue.

"There's plenty of evening left for that," Afton waved off Skye's concern, as Knox and Bella went into the living room.

"So where've you been?" Afton asked her sister.

Skye paused for a several seconds. "At the park, just out there walking the trail. And thinking."

Afton stopped and stared. "Are you okay?"

"I had a doctor's appointment today."

Afton immediately assumed there would be no more babies. Skye's reproductive years were likely behind her. She had been hopeful though. She really wanted her sister to have another child. Bella was precious, and everyone loved her and doted on her. To see her grow with a sibling would have completed their family. She knew how much Skye had wanted another baby, just lately, as she had felt so strongly about Bella having a little brother or sister to grow up with and to navigate her life with.

"I'm guessing it didn't go well. You know, you could use two donors, or look into adoption. Bella can still have a sibling if you want that badly enough for her."

"My eggs are healthy," Skye stated as a matter of fact.

"Oh. Well good! Then what's wrong?" Afton was beginning to worry.

Knox walked back into the room. He took one look at the women in front of him and then started to back away. He knew he had interrupted.

"Wait. Knox, please stay. I would like to talk to you both." She watched him swap a glance with Afton. "Something's happened. I've thought about this, and I need to share it with you both. I've changed my mind. I want a baby of my own and if you, both of you," Afton looked at Knox initially, and then at her sister, "are in this with me, I want Knox to father a baby brother or sister for Bella." It was the most appropriate way to word it. *She wanted Knox to father a sibling for Bella. She didn't say that she wanted Knox to be the father of her child.*

Knox was taken aback. He again had convinced himself that becoming a father would never happen for him.

Afton stepped toward her sister and enveloped her in her arms. Skye tried so very hard to fight back the tears, but it was like a dam had broken and she started to sob in Afton's embrace.

"Those better be happy tears," Afton teased her, as they pulled out of each other's arms, and turned to Knox. His eyes were teary too. He never moved from where he stood. He was too afraid that if he stirred, he would wake up and discover this was just another dream. His nonverbal reaction conveyed just how much he wanted this chance.

"So, what do you say, Knox? Ready to get knocked up in a lab?"

Afton may have laughed the loudest at that awkward comment, which was probably best because Knox could only think of what it was going to be like to hold his own child. And Skye was focused on knowing that one day she would have to ask them both if they would not only raise Knox's baby — but Bella too. They could be a family. Skye would leave her children behind to be loved and protected by them. It was the only answer. She would lose her mind if she did not have this vision, this plan in place, for her child — or likely, children.

"You changed your mind," Knox said to Skye. "Why?"

"Because I can't do this alone. I've done it with Bella, and with the help of my sisters I've survived. I want more than that for another child. This baby will need a father, just like Bella needs you at times now." Afton was surprised by Skye's words. "All I mean by that is, you both love her and are there for her. So I can only imagine a new baby in the mix."

"You don't have to do this alone," Afton reached for Skye's hand, and she choked on a sob.

"Thank you. Thank you both so very much." Skye made genuine, grateful eye contact with Knox while she stood near her sister. Eventually they would know how much this truly meant to her.

Chapter 13

*S*orry *I missed your text and couldn't help with Bella. It was a hectic evening at school. So glad to send off this class. They were hellish.*

Laney sent that message to Skye after 9 p.m. She stood in her kitchen, and stared at the closed refrigerator door. Three days. She made it three days without drinking any alcohol. She purposely had not bought any wine when she was at the grocery store picking up dinner ingredients last night. She chided herself now for not even getting just one bottle. It was graduation tonight! A justifiable reason to celebrate!

Her phone dinged to alert her of a text message. Skye replied.

It all worked out. Knox rescued Bella for me. Good to know those hellish kids moved on. Haha.

It was amazing how Knox had quickly become a trusted part of the family, Laney thought.

Skye wasn't prepared to get into this tonight. And the shock of this would probably be inappropriate to communicate by text message. She relented and called Laney.

"You need to hear this from me." Those were Skye's first words the moment Laney answered her call.

"Okay, just tell me."

"Are you sitting down with a drink in your hand?"

"No." *And please don't remind me of that little voice in my head that needs one. Just one drink. Jesus. It would be harmless.*

"I've decided to have another baby. Still no surrogate, but I do have a baby daddy." Laney waited. She was instantly worried for what this meant. She knew before Skye confirmed it. "Knox agreed to do this with me, and of course you know Afton is completely supportive. It was, after all, her initial idea!" Laney didn't want to crush her sister's excitement, *but what had changed? Why did they think this would ever work when just days ago there were so many reasons not to do it? How did Skye, especially, go from seriously unsettled to completely at ease about this?*

"You're not saying anything," Skye broke Laney's silence. "Are you tipping back the Moscato for the courage to speak your mind in a moment."

"No, damn it! I'm not! And stop referring to my drinking."

Unseen, Skye's eyes widened on her end of the phone. "Okay, sorry. I was just teasing. I know how much you like a cocktail at the end of the day, that's all."

"It's fine. You're fine. I'm just edgy." *Because she needed a drink to take that edge off!* "And I don't need courage to tell my own sister that I think she is making a mistake."

Before her (still unofficial) health crisis diagnosis, Skye might have agreed with her. But now everything had changed. She desperately needed Knox. And Afton. "I know we can make this work. Please just support me, all of us. We're family. We've finally gotten close, and are about to get closer, I hope. Doesn't a baby do that?"

Laney muffled a sigh. "I just hope you know what you're doing. This is on you if Afton and Knox begin to have relationship problems. I will give you my full support. I love this family as we are, and I will be nothing but supportive and encouraging about this even though you have done a complete 180 for reasons unknown to me!"

"Are you angry?" Skye asked, cautiously.

"No. And I do appreciate knowing this. You know how I hate to be the last one to know."

"Well, technically, you are..."

"Just know I'm flipping you off right now."

"Good. That's what sisters do. I love you, Laney." Skye's eyes were instantly teary as she spoke. She would miss this someday, wherever she was going.

"I love you back, sis."

Dr. Dylan Freund was not what Skye expected. She visualized a man past his prime, seasoned in the medical field and well-educated on how to put up a good fight against blood cancer. She chided herself for that callous thought. He wasn't well past his prime. If Skye had to guess, Dr. Fruend was likely in his early forties. He was only an inch or two taller than her, so she guessed he was under six-foot. Beneath that white lab coat, from what Skye could tell, he was in great shape. Broad, thick chest. Tight, muscular upper arms. His perfectly round head was completely clean shaven. Without hair, his bright blue eyes were prominent. His voice was low and soft at the same time. Soothing was a fitting descriptive word.

He had a plan in place for Skye. She was at a loss for words as he explained, in detail, that yes, she did have blood cancer. Myeloma, Stage 1.

There were three stages, and the higher the stage, the poorer the outcome. There also were different forms of myeloma-related conditions. Some required treatment, some did not. Those affected by the disease required regular check-ups to monitor the progression of the disease.

Skye also learned that the disease was classified into Group A or Group B, based on damage to the kidneys. She was considered Group A because she still had normal kidney function. *Was she supposed to be grateful for that?*

"So what I am hearing is, if I must be burdened with this disease, I am winning with a lesser stage," Skye began, surprised not to hear her own voice sound shaky. She was both afraid and nervous, and as with most things in her life she was initially facing this alone. "Am I right to assume that the cancer was caught in time?" Skye, at this point, had no idea what type of treatments she would have to endure or if the cancer could be kept at bay. She was mindful of this being an incurable type that eventually would progress, but right now she was desperately holding on to this one positive result.

"It was caught at a very early stage," Dr. Fruend confirmed her positivity, "which will allow me to assess whether you even need to begin treatment just yet. Signs and symptoms appear to be null, which in most cases will keep patients from having to begin therapy. Don't misunderstand me though, this is not going to go away. It may lay dormant for a time period, briefly or for several years, but it's there and we need to watch it closely."

Skye didn't say anything else. *It was only a matter of time before her body began to succumb to this disease.* She held tight to the truth that it hadn't yet. *But, the reality was sooner or later she would still die.* She exhaled a long, slow breath. Dylan Fruend wasn't oblivious to her beauty. She looked years younger than her medical chart stated. Her blonde hair was tied back neatly into a simple, low ponytail. This woman, however, was far from ordinary. She had long, shapely legs. A Barbie doll figure, if he had to make a specific comparison. But that patch of freckles across the bridge of her nose though. It made him smile, as it added imperfection to a woman who appeared at first glance to be flawless. It pained him to know that she was seriously ill. No one deserved that cruel kind of unfairness hurled at them. Ever. He saw it every single day in this profession. But there was something about Skye Gallant that caused him to lose sight of the facts. *Incurable. Temporary remission.*

What about those people out there who come along every so often and beat all the odds?

Chapter 14

Laney turned around from the kitchen counter, coffee in hand, taking her first hot sip. Brad was seated at the kitchen table, reading the newspaper. *Did anyone actually read the news in print anymore?* Her husband still did. Luke walked into the room with sleepy eyes and bed head.

"Morning sweetie."

He grunted.

"Did you sleep well?"

"Are you kidding me? Liam coughed half the night. And when he wasn't coughing, he kept making some kind of whistling sound when he breathed." The boys shared a room. Brad knocked a wall out upstairs so the two of them could have one giant room, both with king-size beds. They still, even at thirteen, wanted to be together a lot. Especially when they slept.

"Really? I never heard him. Did you, Brad?" She immediately blamed the allergy season, and turned around to search a makeshift medicine cabinet for an antihistamine.

Brad looked up from the newspaper and nodded his head. "I've told you for decades that you sleep like a rock. "It did get a little annoying," Brad agreed with his son.

"A little? Try being in the same room with him." Luke was toasting two pieces of bread and reached for the peanut butter in a higher cabinet when Laney found the Zyrtec. Liam joined them in the kitchen before she could ask Luke if his brother was awake yet.

"Hey... rough night?" Laney felt a little guilty for not coming to his aide. That's what mothers did. She was, in fact, an incredibly sound sleeper. When the boys were babies, she practically slept with one eye forced open in fear of not hearing them when they needed her. Their hunger cries had been ear piercing though.

"Just a few coughing fits." His voice sounded hoarse as he made fleeting eye contact with her.

"Take one of these with your breakfast," Laney used her finger to tap out a pill from the bottle, onto the counter. And if he didn't get relief, he was going to the doctor. Like it or not.

Two weeks went by and that dry cough had not subsided. Allergies were ruled out by the general practitioner who treated the twins since birth, so a few tests followed. It was concluded that Liam had a bacterial respiratory infection. He was prescribed an antibiotic and a steroid to lessen the inflammation in his lungs. An official diagnosis also followed.

"What is popcorn lung?" Laney asked the doctor while she and Liam sat with him in the examination room of their family physician's office.

They heard the doctor explain that it was a chronic lung disease. He defined it as a rare condition which causes airway scarring due to inflammation and eventually lung damage. Treatments did exist, but there was no cure. And it could be considered life-threatening.

Laney almost turned off her mind to the seriousness of what she heard. *How could this be?* She asked their trusted doctor that very same question.

In return, she heard that possible causes in Liam's case were exposure to toxic fumes or infection. The doctor concluded that Liam's condition was caused by a chemical called diacetyl, which was found in flavored e-cigarettes. Liam had admitted to vaping when the doctor asked him too many questions about his medical history and current activity.

Laney practically held her breath. Or perhaps the shock of what the medical doctor was saying had taken her breath away. *Her son was sick because of something he was purposely doing to himself. He lied to her. He told her he quit vaping weeks ago.* The doctor had said the exposure to the dangerous chemical will slowly worsen the lung-related symptoms over a period of weeks to months. Hence, Liam's persistent cough and wheezing.

She waited until they were alone in the car before she spoke. The shared silence was killing them both. Laney sat behind the wheel with the engine still off. It was hot in there. She reacted and turned the key in the ignition before she powered the air conditioner on full blast. Liam couldn't take it anymore. He wanted her to say something. Anything.

"You're mad at me for vaping," he began. "I said I'd quit, but I didn't. I will now though, I swear. I mean, the doctor said if I stop completely my lungs won't get worse. I'll stop the cause of this, mom. That will help me. Right?"

"You could die," she turned and glared at him with hot tears in her eyes. She wanted to scream at him for how stupid this was for him to even begin experimenting with! But she stopped herself. All those Camels she smoked in high school now burned in her memory. *He was just a kid, making dumb choices. We all did it.* The reality of having to pay such a high price for it, however, was incredibly unfair. But how many times had she lectured him and his brother about the dangers of vaping? There were new findings all the time concerning the risks of the chemicals. *It was worse than smoking an actual cigarette,* one article had stated.

"I'm not though. Right? I'm not going to die, mom." Laney could see the panic in his eyes. He needed her reassurance.

"No. You're not. But you are going to have to see doctors regularly for the rest of your life to keep this condition under control."

"I will, I will, I promise." Her teenage son suddenly didn't sound so grown up.

"I want to be so pissed at you right now," Laney admitted to her son, "but I can't be. I can't be upset and angry over something we cannot change. It's done and over. Just learn from this, Liam. Sometimes our choices in life cannot be taken back. Don't do yourself harm." Those words suddenly tasted bitter in her mouth, but she had to say them. This needed to be a lesson learned for her son. Inside her mind though was a tiny little voice on repeat reminding her that she often times drank too much. Alcohol abuse was an addiction, just like nicotine.

She reached for her son. Liam grasped her hand. And then he bent forward and fell apart in the passenger seat of their car like a frightened, ashamed child. Laney didn't hesitate. She turned her body into him and held him as tightly as she possibly could with her own tears streaming down her cheeks.

Chapter 15

Laney finished her second glass of wine in the company of her sisters. She cried when she explained how Liam had airway scarring in his lungs from the persistent vaping. Popcorn lung was a rare condition and the existing inflammation in his lungs would cause permanent damage. At thirteen years old, Liam was no longer a healthy boy. And Laney was having a difficult time grasping that truth.

Skye, for once, wasn't the first to respond. She sat back and listened while Afton had numerous questions about the condition being life threatening. *Would he need a lung transplant in years to come?* She thought of her own devastating diagnosis that she continued to keep to herself. Skye would tell them, eventually. She had to. But first, Skye wanted to plan for her daughter's future without interference from anyone. She would not be swayed from her plan to have another child.

"It sounds as if Liam can get this condition under control and live a full, productive life, correct?" Skye finally spoke.

That's the way I understand it, too," Laney answered her. "He wheezes at times and he has a nagging dry cough. Sometimes people with this experience shortness of breath or difficulty breathing deeply with physical activity. Those are things we can expect, but may or may not see in Liam. We really don't know exactly how he will be affected."

"It could be worse then," Afton added.

"Why do people say that?" Skye spoke up, and her tone made both of her sisters turn and attempt to read her abrupt reaction. "I mean, really, it's your own pain. Worse or better has nothing to do with it."

"It's just a way to remain positive and optimistic," Afton defended.

"I see both sides of it actually," Laney partially agreed with both of them. "My son is no longer the same. He's plagued with something that will change his life. That sucks for him and for me as his mother. Could it be worse? Absolutely. It could also be a hell of a lot better, as in, I want my completely healthy kid back."

"We can't turn back time or change things," Skye stated from personal experience more than anyone realized. "Take this in stride, and trust that he is going to be okay. None of us know how much time we have." Life was fleeting and unpredictable. And incredibly unfair. Both Laney and Afton believed Skye was referring to how suddenly they lost their mother. This time, however, it was even more personal. She was reeling from the shock of her own health crisis.

"Just remember what life has taught us," Afton began. "The Gallant sisters are stronger together." Skye felt her eyes get teary. And Laney took a generous swallow from her wine glass.

"I have some news," Skye spoke. She paused to clear her throat before she became too emotional. "Three of my eggs have been removed and reserved. I'm told I have healthy, normal eggs."

Afton immediately reached for Skye's hand across the table. They were in Laney's kitchen. "You didn't tell us. I would have been there for you for the procedure. Skye, you do not have to do this alone." *Yes, she did. At least until she knew that no one could talk her out of anything.*

"There will be plenty of things ahead that I'll want you to be a part of with me. Knox too," Skye added.

Afton smiled. "He's beside himself with excitement and joy."

Skye giggled. "As he should be. He's preparing to be a daddy."

Laney kept silent. She still did not see this as something that would work. At least not flawlessly.

"So, tell me. What happens next?" Afton's excitement instantly unnerved Laney. This wasn't a party they were planning. This was the conception of a baby in a lab. A baby that Skye would share with their sister's lover, or life partner, or whatever they were calling him now.

"We need to find a surrogate. And then Knox will have to give his sample."

"Okay I really don't want to have that vision in my mind right now," Laney rolled her eyes.

Skye smirked. Afton laughed

"I plan to help him with that... you know, to be a part of this." Afton surprisingly had not felt the least bit awkward sharing that.

"Do what you need to do," Skye smiled at her. "Just bottle the goods from my baby daddy." They giggled, with the exception of Laney, who stood up to refill her wine glass again. She could not be a part of that exchange. She feared her sisters would never be this close again. *That baby they were planning was going to eventually drive a rift between them.*

Laney embraced a familiar feeling of freedom that made its way into her life at the end of every month of May when the school year concluded. She was still in her classroom, gathering a few things at her desk to bring home for the summer break, when her student teacher came back through the open classroom door.

"Savannah? Hey, I thought you left?" Laney always grew attached to her student teachers, who were typically young college-age students. Savannah, however, was thirty years old. She went to college later, once she decided on a career path that felt right for her. Thirty was still young, and Laney was a little envious of her lack of responsibilities. No husband. No children. She was only committed to beginning a new career, hopefully as a middle school science teacher as soon as the next school year began in the fall.

"I did, but I came back to talk to you about something. I guess you could say I needed to work up the courage." Laney turned from her desk to look at Savannah. She was short, barely five-foot, three. Her body was petite, but muscular. She looked like a runner, or someone who worked out regularly. Her dark hair was knotted high on her head in a ponytail.

"Courage? It's just me. I think we've gotten to know each other pretty well these last four months."

Savannah nodded her head in agreement. "That's why I'm going to just come right out and ask you this. When we said our goodbyes earlier, you mentioned if I ever needed anything, I should—"

"Just ask?" Laney smiled as she finished her sentence. She could write her a letter of recommendation, or talk to anyone on her behalf. Laney was certain someone would immediately hire her.

Savannah inhaled a deep breath. "I was on your computer a few days ago, and the search history came up. I didn't want to say anything at first, but now I do, because it feels like it was a sign of some sort. I never told you this, because I really don't just go around telling people, but I want you to know something. I think if you knew my situation, you would allow me to help." Laney had absolutely no idea what Savannah was referring to. She waited for her to explain. "Three years ago, I did something that I felt in my heart was the right thing to do. I was almost twenty-seven years old, I had started college on this path to teach and I really needed the money..."

Laney forced her facial expression not to change. She would hear her out and not be shocked or judge her in any way. The two of them had gotten close, teaching together in her classroom the entire semester, but whatever was on Savannah's mind right now was past the point of serious.

"I saw that you searched for information on surrogacy."

Laney let out a sigh. "Oh...yeah that." She was not at all in agreement with Skye and Afton, but she had attempted to research surrogates in the Twin Cities. It's not like she wanted to help. On a whim, Laney was just looking to gain knowledge of a subject that would quickly become personal for her family. But it didn't matter what Laney learned. Skye was likely many steps ahead of her anyway. "My sister is considering having a second baby with the help of a surrogate." She left out the part where her other sister's lover would be the sperm donor.

"Your sister," Savannah spoke.

"You thought it was me?" Laney laughed. "Have you not heard my cries for help as I parent my teenage boys?" She laughed again.

"How serious is your sister?" Savannah inquired.

"Very serious, I believe."

"Laney, I was a surrogate, and it was an incredible experience for me," Savannah admitted. "I was able to help nurture a life as it grew inside of me, and then I gave birth to someone else's dream. I want to do that again. It's such a miracle." She paused. "I would love for that to be for your sister, if she has not found anyone yet."

Laney backed up and sat down on the edge of her desk. She, at first, didn't have the words. "Wow. I don't know what to say. I mean, how selfless of you." Earnings or not, that was quite the sacrifice with someone's own body. "I really don't know how far my sister has gotten with her search for a surrogate." She would find out though. While Laney certainly had not planned to play any significant role in this plan of her sisters, she recognized that she could have a purpose in this now. *Was this really some kind of sign? Was this her mother guiding her from beyond?* It felt strange for Laney to rally for this now, when she still believed it would be a mistake.

Chapter 16

Have you gotten serious about finding a surrogate yet?

That was the text message Laney sent to Skye. She debated whether or not to include Afton, but didn't. Not yet.

A few minutes later, Laney's phone rang.

"That's a pretty loaded question to ask me by text," Skye stated when Laney answered.

"Right. Sorry. I didn't know if you were too busy to talk."

"Not too busy." Skye had actually been asleep. She laid down with Bella for a nap. She had been doing more of that lately to save her strength. If she was sick, she needed to take care of her body. Dr. Fruend had reminded her of that at her last visit. "Why do you ask though?" Skye and Afton both knew Laney was not completely on-board with their plan to bring a baby into this world with Knox. She initially had expressed her disapproval when she said, *some things were just too close for comfort.* And Laney was indeed worried about the connection that would forever form between Skye and Knox if they shared a child.

Laney paused. She didn't know if she should delve into this over the phone. "I wondered if you had gone through specific ropes with an agency or something to find a surrogate, or where you would even begin."

"In my research and after talking to my doctor at length about it, I discovered that you can go through an agency, or choose not to. Sometimes people use someone they know. Unfortunately my process is already harder and will take a little longer because I don't have that leisure. I can't hardly ask it as a favor to someone I know."

"I could probably save you that considerable time and effort," Laney began.

"Explain what you mean," Skye suddenly found herself pacing through her living room. Time was of the essence for this pregnancy. Finding the right surrogate was a task that overwhelmed her right now. She had spent countless hours researching and learning the pros and cons of the entire process. The screening part worried her. She didn't want to trust just anyone — even if an agency approved of her. *But if Laney could help...*

"This is going to sound strange, but I may have found a woman who could be the right fit to carry your baby. I've just spent the last sixteen weeks with a student teacher in my classroom, and I had no idea until today that she had been a surrogate before. Her name is a Savannah Emig. She's thirty years old. I know you will need more than just my word, but she's a lovely, compassionate and selfless person."

"She's been a surrogate before?"

"Yes... and she approached me about this subject after she used my computer and randomly came across a previous search I did on a whim for surrogacy. Skye... she wants to do this again. She called the experience the first time a true miracle."

"I want to meet her as soon as possible!" Skye's pulse was racing.

"I can arrange that." Laney smiled.

"Lane? Are you okay with this?"

"I would not have brought this up if I wasn't." That wasn't entirely true. But she needed to be supportive. This was, after all, her family. And now Laney may have just found a way to give her sisters the gift of the perfect surrogate. This wasn't too good to be true. This was the way life worked when the stars were aligned, and something was supposed to happen. Laney truly believed that.

"Do you know what this could mean?" Skye was beyond hopeful. She trusted both of her sisters above anyone else. If Laney believed in this woman, she would too.

"Yes." Laney couldn't deny that she felt this in her heart. "Savannah was led to you through me. This is a higher power at work... or mom," she giggled.

Skye smiled into the phone. "Let's do this."

In vitro fertilization was most definitely a true miracle. It made it possible to gather a healthy, reproductive egg from Skye, fertilize it with sperm from Knox, and then the embryo was placed into the uterus of a gestational surrogate named Savannah. In nine months, Skye and Knox would share a child.

Chapter 17

"I feel a little guilty having a drink in front of you," Laney spoke honestly to her friend, Savannah, as she sipped a glass of white wine with her salad.

Savannah waved a hand in front of her face. "Oh please. It really doesn't even faze me. I'm not much of a drinker anyway."

Every few weeks, Laney had a lunch date with Savannah. It was a chance for them to stay in touch since they were no longer working together — and even more importantly, Savannah was carrying Laney's niece or nephew in that expanding pooch of hers. She was two months pregnant.

Laney smiled. "So how many minutes has it been since my sister called you last?"

Savannah reacted with a giggle before she spoke. "Which one?"

"Is Afton as bad as Skye?"

"She's calling on behalf of Knox, she says." Savannah winked.

"Does that drive you crazy?"

"Not at all," Savannah answered, honestly. "I'm carrying their baby. They have every right to check on us."

"Us," Laney laughed. "How cute…"

"That's how Skye always puts it. She wants us both to have everything we need. I could not ask for better, more caring, parents to work for."

"That's wonderful to hear, thank you," Laney stabbed a forkful of lettuce on her plate and put it in her mouth after she spoke. She politely held up her napkin to her mouth while she chewed and spoke again. "So are those two still serious about not finding out the gender?"

"That's what they say," Savannah giggled. "They certainly aren't typical parents nowadays."

Laney laughed out loud as she swallowed some more wine. "Typical is far from their situation, and our family in general!"

Savannah smiled. "I think it's a wonderful story of love and sacrifice. Skye is doing this for her daughter, and Afton wants the man she loves to have the one thing she cannot give him. Ahhh… what I wouldn't give to find a love like theirs."

"Well you've put yourself off the market for several months now," Laney stated, referring to the pregnancy.

"Right," Savannah laughed. "I'll get back in the game after that."

"Do you worry about telling a man in your life one day that you went through two pregnancies for babies that were not your own? I mean, not everyone can accept or understand something like that."

"I know what you're saying but, if and when I find the right man, that shouldn't matter. Or, it should be viewed as a positive thing. Being a surrogate has been a huge part of my adult life."

"You're a gift to my family, Savannah. We will always be here for you, please know that."

Dr. Fruend straddled a low stool directly in front of Skye, who sat on the exam table and dangled her long legs in front of him. As a doctor, he was focused on his patient. As a man, he noticed those long, shapely legs.

"As your doctor, it's my job to find the best treatment option to fit your needs," he began, and Skye listened raptly. Once a month she had blood drawn and tested. This was her second month seeing Dr. Fruend regularly. "My goal is to get my patients into remission."

"Are you saying something has changed with my blood work since last month?" Skye held her breath.

"No. That's just it. It hasn't, and so I will treat this as if you are in remission — until something changes."

"Until I have what would be the equivalent of a relapse, even though I have yet to be sick."

Dr. Fruend smirked a little. She continued to speak as if everyone, including him, was wrong about her diagnosis. He couldn't explain the slow progression of the myeloma for Skye, but he liked what he saw when he read the results of her last two blood draws. The levels of her blood had not worsened "So absolutely no change in how you feel?"

"I'm tired, but I have a two and half year old." Skye did have a loss of appetite lately, but she forced herself to eat as normal because she did not want to lose weight. She needed what she already carried to fight this battle. She refrained from sharing that information with him.

"Right," he said. "And you're a single mother, correct?" That didn't pertain to her medically, but Dylan Fruend defended how he oftentimes got to know a few personal things about his patients through conversation in order to better understand and help them. Knowing the stress level of his patients was pertinent to him for their well-being.

"I am. I have a little girl, Bella... and a baby on the way actually." Skye didn't think it was a big deal for her doctor to know that. She did what she wanted to do with her life, and couldn't have cared less about the feedback or judgement from others. But she did giggle to herself once she spoke and realized how that sounded. *She was not pregnant.*

Dr. Freund tugged at the stethoscope that hung around the back of his neck and draped forward over his shoulders. "Come again?"

Skye laughed out loud. The kind of laughter that reached her eyes. He noticed that sort of thing about her. She had her genuine moments among displaying that tough girl image. "I probably shouldn't have said that. What I meant was, I need to clarify. I am bringing a second child into the world, with the help of a surrogate."

"Ah, I see," he responded as if he understood, but his mind was reeling. "So was this child on the way before your diagnosis?" That was the only reasonable explanation. He immediately sympathized with Skye. And he speculated... *had she known she was sick...she may not have brought another child into this world.*

"I wanted to do this. I wanted a second child, via surrogate. Even after you told me that I have blood cancer and my chances of living a long, full life became slimmer than I want them to be, I still went ahead with the in vitro."

"Why?" This wasn't Dr. Fruend that she was talking to anymore. Skye could feel the change in him. He was easy to talk to, as a friend too. Even if he was the doctor sitting in front of her in a white lab coat, balancing an iPad on his lap with her personal blood tests results glaring back at him.

"I wanted a sibling for my daughter, someone she can share her entire life with. Parents don't outlive their kids, or they shouldn't, but in my case, well, you know. I'm doing this for Bella. Knowing that I'm sick doesn't change anything. In fact, it's a comfort to know my children will have each other... after I'm gone." Those words were harder for Skye to choke out.

Selfless. This woman was definitely that. "You're a beautiful person," he spoke, and caught himself. His face and bald head flushed momentarily, and Skye grinned to herself. "What I meant was… that's a beautiful thing you are doing. None of us know how long we have on this earth. We want to soak up anything and everything that makes *us* happy. We get upset when we don't have what *we* want, or when we know things are not going to go our way. You're forging ahead for your child, I mean, your children."

"Don't get me wrong, doctor. I know how to complain with the best of them."

They both laughed.

When she called him *doctor*, he was sort of snapped back to the reality of this woman, sitting casually right there in front of him, being his patient.

But, as Skye remarked, he hadn't gotten her wrong, or misjudged her. *Not at all.*

Chapter 18

Dylan Fruend's physician's office was located on the grounds of Regency Memorial. There were other medical buildings surrounding the hospital as well. Skye's gynecologist was also conveniently located there. The parking lots were adjoined and shared between the hospital and the medical buildings. Skye had to park her jeep at the far end of the parking lot closest to the building where she had an appointment with Dr. Fruend. In a hurry and running late, Skye just parked in the first available spot and walked the distance. She was back at the parking space again now, and in the process of getting into her jeep. Her blonde hair was blowing in the wind, as she had it down today. It was her hair and her unmistakable tan legs in those short white shorts, that caught his eye first, as he was leaving the hospital.

People parked anywhere in those available lots. But, to Knox, it looked like Skye had come from the direction of the oncologist's office. His first obvious thought was she was working. He of course initially met Skye when she was in the hospital corridors on her way to a website design meeting. *That was likely it.* Knox dismissed any further thoughts. And before he could catch her attention, she was gone. He would mention that he saw her the next time they were together.

Afton walked into Robertson Funeral Home, located downtown Saint Paul. It felt strange to her because it was vacant and eerily quiet. She stood just a few feet from the front door until she spotted Jess rounding the corner. "Oh thank God! Can we get out of here?"

Jess giggled. She understood that people were uncomfortable in that element. And she could relate to Afton's mindset about simply being there. "I get it. You're not okay with being here."

"It's so different when no one is around." It brought her back to when she and Jess were alone in the morgue with Sam's body. They weren't in the basement now, but in any case they were still under that same roof. She needed to pull herself together. "I really don't know how you can function here."

Jess rolled her eyes. She had certainly gotten used to it by now. "I'm working. And besides, I've always been fascinated with Mark's business." And soon it would be hers.

"I'm happy for you, but can we go? Or I can wait for you outside?"

"You really are edgy," Jess told her, as they both heard the high-pitched beep of the security system to alert that the back door had been opened.

"What's that?"

"The back door. It's likely just Patrick." A second later, they both heard him call out Jess' name.

"In the foyer..." she raised her voice in response.

Patrick wore a dark suit with a paisley gray tie. He was at least ten years younger than Jess and Afton. He carried himself well. The product in his black hair gave it a wet look. His boyish face was clean shaven and he had a visible dimple on his chin. He was tall, at least two inches taller than Jess in high heels. He definitely was handsome, and Afton felt like he knew it. There was an arrogance about him.

"Oh hello. Afton Drury, right?"

Afton nodded her head. "Hi Patrick, how are you doing?"

Patrick extended his hand to hers. "Very well, thank you. And you?"

"Wonderful. I just stopped by to steal Jess away for lunch."

"Great. I need to be at a funeral in Minneapolis. I just stopped in to grab something." Afton watched him eye Jess. It was like one of those times when only a couple people in the room knew what was going on. Afton was the odd woman out right now. She could feel it.

"Did you need me for something?" Jess really didn't want to give up her lunch date with Afton.

"No. You're fine. I was going to ask you to make a few calls for me, but that can wait. Go. Enjoy. I'll catch up with you later. It was nice to see you, Afton." Patrick smiled at them both and took a few steps backwards before he turned the corner.

Afton stared at Jess.

"What?" she whispered and felt slightly annoyed because she knew what Afton was thinking. That conversation would continue outside in Jess' vehicle.

Afton buckled her seatbelt in the passenger seat of Jess' black Escalade. Jess always drove. She preferred to, so Afton never argued. "You're sleeping with him," Afton spoke outright. Their friendship had come a long way. There were no boundaries between them anymore. No words or actions that were phony or pretentious.

Jess had her eyes on the road, but she turned to Afton momentarily. "I am not."

"Are you lying to me?"

"We don't do that to each other anymore," Jess spoke, and she sounded so sincere that Afton was touched. "I told you, there's some serious chemistry between us and I'm fighting it because I don't want to make that mistake with my life again."

Afton thought of her late husband, Sam — and how the two of them had a long, on-going affair that no one knew about. Not even Afton for many years. Afton agreed, the sexual tension was thick. "What are you going to do? You have to work with him."

"I'm going to stay focused on my work," Jess spoke as a matter of fact.

"He seems arrogant, or did I read that wrong?"

"He's sure of himself. He's kind and compassionate to our clients. He's a good listener. He doesn't make everything about himself. I think the arrogance is a facade when he's uncomfortable. He was probably a little nervous around one of Saint Paul's finest businesswomen."

Afton laughed out loud. "You're full of it."

"I'm serious! Look at yourself and your life. You've got it together. Ever since you met Knox, you have a new confidence. Not that there wasn't any there before, it's just different. It's captivating for me to watch how you've changed."

"What? I think you're just talking to hear yourself talk. I'm still me."

"Of course you are, but livelier."

They both laughed.

When they sat down in a booth at their favorite Mexican restaurant, Jess slid a menu toward Afton. While the waiter was at their table, Jess asked Afton outright, "Are we drinking with lunch?"

Afton nodded. "Yes, please."

"Margaritas on the rocks, classic, and hold the salt please." Jess ordered for them. And when the waiter left, she spoke to Afton. "So you know all there is to know about my life, currently. I study. I work. I'm extremely sex deprived but I fight the overwhelming urge to lift my skirt for another married man. Your turn. What's the latest with the surrogate?" Jess did not agree with what they were doing. She believed Afton was going to end up regretful and heartbroken. She hoped though, for her best friend's sake, that she was wrong.

Once the waiter came back with their drinks, Afton was giggling behind the rim of her glass. "I know it's not funny, and I don't want you to be deprived of anything, really. Just the way you described yourself now, it gave me the giggles."

Jess winked at her. "Stop laughing at me, and talk to me. Is Knox beside himself, knowing he's going to finally be a daddy?"

Afton smiled. "He is. I think the time is going too slow for him. He wants that baby to be here now."

"And what about you?"

"I'm grateful to be able to make this happen for him. Yes, it was my initial idea, and Knox and Skye definitely know they have my blessing. I want this as much as they do, just in a different way."

"What happens when Knox's life is consumed with his child?"

Afton paused to choose her words carefully. "I know that's what everyone is thinking. Will this baby end what Knox and I share? I hope with all of my heart that I never have to face the day without that man. He knows how I feel. We are confident that our relationship is healthy and strong, and we are ready to seize life and its challenges together. He needs this child, and I simply want that for him."

Jess watched Afton take a long drink of her margarita, and she lifted her own glass. "To you... Cheers to the most selfless woman I know and love."

Afton smiled, and clinked her glass with Jess'. "You, my friend, are equally as special to me. I love you endlessly, and I need you in my life. To us!"

"As we are!" Jess proclaimed.

"Right. Who else would indulge in tequila together at ten minutes before noon?"

Chapter 19

They should have stopped drinking after two glasses each. Instead, it was three...or was it four glasses? Five. It was five.

Luckily the funeral home was only a few blocks away. Driving intoxicated was a huge risk no matter the distance. They made it though. Jess was able to focus and get them back there safely.

"I don't want to be back here," Afton whined, as they attempted to gracefully stagger together, arms linked, into the foyer.

"Oh quit your fussing, I have work to do. And you need to sober up before you drive home. Or should we call Knox?"

"No need for that! I can take care of myself. A glass of water would help."

Jess nodded. "That's exactly what we need!"

They were in the kitchenette. Afton had the freezer door open on the refrigerator, and she had her head stuck inside. She took deep breaths. "I am so wasted."

Jess laughed at her. "Does that help? Hey, move over, I want to try that!"

Afton barely moved over an inch or two when Jess pushed her way in. Both of their heads were in the freezer. They were giggling at how ridiculous it was when Patrick walked in and he saw them. He had a puzzled look on his face for a moment, and then he realized they were tipsy. Or possibly past that point.

"Hello ladies..."

His voice startled them both. They jumped and nearly bumped heads as they hurried to back out of the freezer.

"Patrick!" Jess responded first. "We were just..."

"Sticking our heads in the freezer," Afton finished her sentence. "It helps with hot flashes." They both laughed out loud in unison.

"Right," Patrick grinned. "How much did you two have to drink at lunch?" He could smell the tequila coming out of their pores. "Never mind. Sit. I'll get some water." They needed to hydrate and flush the toxins from their bodies.

"Well aren't you the sweetest, taking care of us like this," Afton watched Jess take ahold of Patrick's paisley gray tie and she ran her fingers down the length of it on his chest and almost down to his belt buckle. Afton's eyes widened. She was sober enough to see that Jess was flirting. *Dangerously.*

"I'm happy to help," Patrick touched her hand to his chest.

Damn it. No. Afton needed to remind Jess what she was doing before she did it.

"I'll bet you are. It's been a looong time since I let a man take care of me, if you know what I mean..." Patrick chuckled. Afton suddenly snapped completely out of her drunken state, as Jess kept rambling. "Yes, it has. Not since Sam..."

Afton nearly choked on the water she had just tipped to her mouth. "You meant Mark, honey!" she instantly intervened.

"Oh. Right. I meant Mark. I'm so drunk I can't get my names straight." Jess tried to cover for herself.

"Wasn't Sam *your* husband?" Patrick asked Afton.

"He was," Afton nodded.

"And he went missing?"

"He did." Afton could have cursed their carelessness today. Drinking brought their walls down. They never should have come back to the funeral home. She still felt like Jess was not in control of her spoken words, or her actions.

"So did they ever solve his missing person's case? I mean, do the police think he's dead? It's not my intention to disrespect him or you, but it's been like a year, hasn't it?"

"Not quite a year," Afton was trying to figure out how to veer away from this subject. "No one knows if he's alive or dead. It's painful, so I'd rather not keep talking about it if you don't mind."

"Of course. I understand." He still, however, looked like he wanted to dig deeper with questions or assumptions.

Afton eyed Jess. "Go with me to the ladies room."

"What? Here?" Jess laughed at her.

"Yes, here. Come on. I don't know my way around this place." Afton pulled Jess by the hand, and Patrick stood back and watched them leave the kitchenette.

When they were behind the closed door in the restroom, Afton spoke firmly. "You need to get a grip. Splash some damn water on your face or something!"

"That was not good. I almost slipped up when I said Sam's name."

"You did slip up! No more. And do not let Patrick ask any further questions. You piqued his curiosity. I could see it!"

"Me too. I'll be careful. I could distract him with sex..."

"Jess!"

"I was kidding..."

"No you weren't."

She wasn't.

"We have to leave. Go home, Jess."

"I will. It's all fine. Don't worry. I have a clear head now."

But Afton doubted that was entirely true. Jess may have sobered up, but she was still a lonely woman.

Knox laughed at her when Afton tried to explain why she and Jess had gotten drunk at lunchtime. "It certainly wasn't intentional. We were just enjoying ourselves... and well, one drink led to another. I don't remember the last time I was so careless like that."

"Well you shouldn't have drove home, but sometimes we all just have to let loose."

"You're right." But Jess had been a little too loose with Patrick when she came onto him and when she accidentally mentioned Sam.

"But?" Knox knew her well.

Afton paused. The two of them shared everything. All of their innermost thoughts and feelings. Nothing was private or a secret, except for what happened to Sam. "We talked a little about Sam tonight," Afton sort of admitted.

Knox paused. If Afton was referring to his disappearance, this was not something he had to know. He of course was curious, but he and Afton had already agreed that this was her secret, and if she never wanted to tell him, she didn't have to. But now it seemed as if she implied that she wanted to talk about it. "Painful memories?" he asked.

"Yeah. Ones that I would like to forget, for sure."

"Then do. Just don't think or speak of it. It's that simple. You have a new life now, with me. Move forward." A part of Knox really did not want to know what happened.

"I'm grateful for that. And for you." Afton leaned in to kiss him.

"You taste like a margarita," he chuckled, and then deepened his kiss.

"Thirsty?" she asked, with her lips on his.

"Maybe..."

And this was their story. One of solid trust, true love, and fiery passion. While Afton was in the arms of a man who had quickly become a familiar safe haven to her, Jess was across town falling back into an old way with a new lover as she inevitably surrendered to the overwhelming lust she felt for Patrick Robertson.

Chapter 20

Regency Memorial's 52nd Annual Ball was a special black-tie gala that featured cocktails, dinner and dancing. Each year, members of the medical staff rotated turns hosting the event. Typically, they paired two staff members for hosting duties and a slew of others, including members of the hospital board, were involved with planning and organizing the important evening. The event celebrated the achievements of the past year, and it provided an opportunity for the community to support a prominent hospital in the Twin Cities.

Knox researched the details of the event from past years. Last year, alone, $10 million was raised for the hospital and those funds helped purchase new cardiac monitoring equipment. Sponsorship opportunities were available for the event, and tickets were $300 per person. Knox took note how the board wanted to increase that price, but did not have enough votes to make the change. Most of the staff groaned about the mandatory involvement in the annual fund raiser, but Knox was all in. He had co-hosted the event eight years ago, and was chosen to do so again. Staff from the surrounding practices in Minneapolis also were involved, including the obstetrician and oncologist offices. Dr. Dylan Fruend was selected to co-host with Knox this year. He knew of him as the notable hemoglobin oncologist on the hospital grounds. Knox had already received an email from him, suggesting they meet to get organized. And now, Knox had a file in hand to deliver to his colleague prior to their meeting. It was sort of like pass-the-torch with those files from year to year. Knox had already read them. He walked through the adjoining parking lots. His last appointment was finished, and he was headed home for the day. But first, he dropped by the oncologist's office with the intent to make a quick delivery to the receptionist's desk.

Knox greeted the middle-aged woman whose nametag read Jane. He explained his reason for leaving the file for Dr. Fruend. It was quick and easy and as he turned to leave, the door to one of the exam rooms opened and he saw two people. One was his colleague and the other was Skye.

Knox couldn't conceal the surprise on his face. He shook hands with his colleague. Dr. Fruend immediately addressed their upcoming *gig*, but Knox only paid partial attention to his words. And then he noticed the obvious. Without a word, Skye started to step away. "Take care of yourself, Skye. See you next time." She was his patient, but he truly cared about her. He genuinely wanted the best for all of his patients. It was different with Skye though, and he knew it.

"You too. Thank you." She never looked back.

Knox let her go. He didn't want to embarrass her or himself. Dylan Fruend didn't need to know that they knew each other. Something was wrong. Skye wasn't there for anything work-related. It appeared that she was a patient. And this both confused and scared him.

After several minutes of conversation, Knox left the office building. He walked outdoors, expecting Skye to have floored her jeep out of there minutes ago. Instead, he found her sitting on a bench under a shade tree on the grounds. She was waiting for him.

Knox walked slowly toward her. He could feel his own pulse pounding inside his chest. Skye stayed silent until he was in front of her. "Sit by me, Knox."

He did.

"You know, I saw you a few weeks ago in this parking lot. It looked to me like you had come from the oncologist's office. I was going to mention it to you sometime, but I believed you were working. I mean, who doesn't share with their family something incredibly serious...like, if they are ill?" Knox turned to make direct eye contact with Skye. She was fighting back tears in her eyes. "Tell me what's going on. I don't want to wait to hear it from Afton. I have a right to know. You and I are connected too. We are going to be parents. We are counting on each other, just as our baby —the moment he or she is born— will be depending on us. That was the plan, Skye."

She forced back more tears. She was strong and that wasn't going to alter now. The only thing that would change was this secret was no longer hers. "I will be here for my child for as long as I possibly can." Time was allocated for everyone on this earth. But no one knew exactly how much they had. "In order to find out if I had healthy reproductive eggs, my gynecologist did some blood work. I had abnormal results that led me to Dr. Fruend."

"He specializes in prevention, diagnosis, and treatment of cancer," Knox stated. His voice cracked. He couldn't look at her right now.

"I have myeloma, a rare form of blood cancer."

"Oh God..." Knox swiftly turned to her. He reached for both of her hands with his own. "You've known about this, for what, months? Were we already pregnant?" Those words sounded so personal, and yet they were connected in that way.

"I knew before we found Savannah, or she found us, and she was implanted with our embryo."

"Why? Why did you let us go through with that... if you knew you were sick?"

Skye paused before she answered him. They were still holding hands. Knox didn't know it, but he was such a comfort to her. Just sitting there. Touching her. And listening. "For my little girl. If I'm gone, she's going to need someone by her side. That was my drive all along, even before I knew about the myeloma."

"This concerns me too, and I could be really angry at you right now," Knox didn't have to explain that it was very possible Skye could die and leave him as a single parent.

"I know that. But you've got this. With or without me. You know that as well as I do."

Knox force swallowed the lump in his throat. "You don't look sick. You don't act like you feel weak or rundown? Are you in treatment?" *Damn it. He had so many questions.* "You can't keep doing this by yourself. You are not alone." Knox didn't have to tell Skye that her sisters were going to be livid, and then turn their anger right around and vow to be right by her side through it all.

"Apparently I'm a puzzling patient for Dr. Fruend. I don't feel sick. My levels, the past three blood draws, have not changed. I have cancer, but it's lying dormant or something."

"As if you're in remission?"

"Yes, exactly. But this is an incurable cancer. It's known to go into remission and then rebound." *She didn't want to say with a vengeance, because she didn't know that for sure. Many people who suffered from myeloma lived for decades, or so she had learned from her research.* "My case is just an unusual one, so far." Knox was hung up on the word *incurable*. He despised it. That was likely why he chose to be an orthopedic surgeon. He could fix bones, muscles, and tendons. They would eventually mend.

"How often do you see Dr. Fruend?"

"Once a month, unless something changes. I have strict orders to call him, STAT." She smiled. She was grateful to have a wonderful, caring physician by her side.

"He's good. One of the best." Knox obviously wanted Skye to be in top-notch medical hands.

"So when are you going to force me to tell my sisters this god-awful news? I don't want to tear them up inside. This will break their hearts." Skye could not imagine being in their place and knowing she was going to lose one of them. But she did want them to hear this news from her. It was time.

"The three of you have something special," Knox began. "Those kinds of relationships are designed to handle both trials and triumphs."

"I believe that now. But I want all of you to understand that this is my life and the decisions ahead that I make will be what I want."

"So what else is new?" Knox said as a matter of fact. "You don't want to be told what to do. We get it. You're a strong, independent woman. You've proved yourself. Now relax and allow other people to help you when you need it. Don't be too proud to admit when life's load is too much. You are only human."

"You think I'm strong?" she asked him. He nodded. "I agree. I am, but do you know what I'm not? Tough. I'm not at all tough. I've never developed a thick skin to protect myself from the hurt. I always wanted to feel it all, you know, life's pleasures and its pains. It's called living. I've always pressed on, no matter what. Because I continuously believed the best was yet to come. At least I trusted it was." This was the first time in her life when Skye wasn't so sure anymore. Some of that hope was lost.

Knox took her hand in his again. She saw the tears in his eyes. His sensitivity warmed her heart. "I am so proud of you." She shook her head and rolled her eyes. "No. Seriously. You are a remarkable woman. You press on and you persevere. Don't let this diagnosis change a thing. You continue to be you."

Skye let a tear escape and trickle down her cheek. She quickly removed her hand from his to brush it away. There was so much more she wanted to say to him, if and when the time came for her to leave this world behind. *Her children needed a daddy. Not just their unborn baby. But Bella too.*

Chapter 21

"I am really worried that there could be something wrong with the baby," Afton spoke what she feared as Laney paced in her and Knox's kitchen. She passed the refrigerator three times, pausing near it every time.

"Savannah hasn't responded to my text to confirm or deny that," Laney said, feeling agitated by Afton's constant implication that there was something terrible happening within their family. Ever since Liam's diagnosis, Laney chose to take life one worry at a time. There was no need to waste negative energy on fretting about something that may or may not happen. "Just wait for Knox and Skye to get here." Knox had sent Afton a text to get Laney over to the house, and said he and Skye would arrive soon. All he conveyed was — Skye needed them.

Laney stood idle near the refrigerator. Afton rolled her eyes. "Just get a drink already. Make yourself at home."

Laney perked up. "Okay. Do you want one too?"

"No."

With that, they both heard car doors outside. "They're here…" Afton spoke and started to bolt out of the kitchen.

"Wait, don't fly out the front door. You know Skye. She likes everything to be on her terms. She's going to get all pissed off and tell you to get your ass back inside the house."

"Right. But she can't keep me from looking out the window!" Afton left the kitchen, while Laney stayed behind to find some chilled alcohol.

From the living room window, Afton called out to Laney. "Skye followed Knox here. She has Bella with her. Knox is getting a stroller out of her jeep." Afton paused. "It looks like he's going to take Bella for a walk."

"Probably to give us time to talk, or Skye the chance to explain what in the hell is going on. I hate how urgent this feels. It makes me nervous." Laney poured a full glass of wine and drank half of it in two gulps before she topped off the glass again.

"What happened to not worrying until you absolutely have to?" Afton was being snarky.

"I'm going to ignore that comment," Laney called back to her.

"Here she comes," Afton stated, and moved toward the front door. Just as Skye opened it, Laney joined them in the living room.

"Hey…" Skye greeted her older sisters. They were her protectors when she was growing up. But they couldn't shield her from this.

"Hey yourself," Laney spoke.

"What's going on?" Afton asked.

"Knox took Bella for a walk so we can talk."

"We're worried something's happened to the baby…" Afton admitted because she wanted instant clarification for that not to be the case. *Why else had Knox been involved?*

"The baby is fine. Last time I checked on Savannah was yesterday." Skye was touched by the concern her sisters already had shown for her unborn child. "No more questions, okay? Let me talk for awhile."

No one sat down. They were never about sitting down to tell each other something outright. *Just say it. Give it to me straight. I can take it.* That's what their mother used to say. And consequently, that was what she taught all three of her girls.

"I'm sick." She didn't know how else to begin. "I had some blood work done before my eggs were retrieved and reserved. The results were abnormal." Afton felt as if she was being thrown into a heavy fog. Her senses seemed blocked. She didn't want to hear any more. And she couldn't see clearly as those stubborn tears clouded her eyes. *She hated to cry!* Laney gripped the stemless wine glass in her hand until her fingers ached. They both did as their little sister asked. They listened. "I was diagnosed by a hemoglobin oncologist with myeloma. It's an incurable blood cancer."

She paused. She watched both Afton and Laney. They stood very still in their respective places. Afton was closest to Skye, and Laney was behind the back of the sectional as she had just come from the kitchen.

"Say something, please, either of you."

"You told us not to!" Laney reacted, and her voice cracked as if she was going to break down.

"How long have you known this?" Afton questioned her, and Skye expected this. She was having the same initial reaction as Knox. *Was the embryo fertilized and implanted before or after this health crisis threatened her life?*

"A few months," Skye answered, honestly, and she heard Laney mumble, *oh my God,* under her breath.

"Why didn't you tell us?" It was an ignorant question, but Afton asked regardless. She had a right to ask. But in her heart Afton knew that Skye was just being Skye. She wanted to shake her for keeping secrets. She always had something to hide. Or at least she used to. Afton chose to believe she had finally grown up and changed and moved past not confiding in them when she was hurting. But that was precisely it. Skye couldn't be forced to make a choice other than what she wanted. She did her own thing at her own damn speed, to her own damn rhythm, and she apologized to no one for it. But Afton could see in her youngest sister's eyes now that she was not completely unfazed by this. Skye had always been the confident sister. But that didn't mean she was immune. She was equally as sensitive as any of them, maybe more. She had just mastered how to better control that sensitivity.

"I don't know how to answer that exactly," Skye admitted. "I suppose I needed time to process this."

"Alone? You can't expect that of yourself. You need us." Laney lectured her. It was easier to be stern right now. It kept her from completely falling apart.

Skye nodded in agreement. "I know you both have a lot of questions. I can answer what I know so far. I've had regular blood tests, three now, since my diagnosis was confirmed, and this cancer is not progressing. Yet. It could though. And it likely will. But my doctor already is labeling this as a remission. It sounds good, I know," she confirmed the positive expressions she saw on their faces, "but myeloma is known for that. The remissions eventually rebound."

"So you're not dying. You could have time, right? Time to raise your babies," Laney stated, and she was almost begging for that reassurance.

"I sure hope so," Skye replied.

"Your babies," Afton repeated. "You went full speed ahead with this plan... Knox, the embryo, the surrogate, the whole shebang. None of us know how long we have here. I don't want you to be sick. I refuse to think about ever losing you." Afton's voice cracked, but she pressed on. She had something more to say. "How is that fair?" Skye knew Afton was referring to everyone who had stake in this. Lives were going to change. They were prepared for that with the unborn baby on its way.

They were not at all prepared, however, for Skye to be living on borrowed time. *Something that she was forewarned about!*

"You want to talk to me about fair?" This was the fighter they recognized. Skye could defend herself and her own actions like no one else. "My little girl could lose her mommy much sooner than the many years down the road that I imagined. She would have to bury me alone. I stand firm in my choice to bring a sibling into this world for my daughter. My children will have each other. I want that comfort embedded in my soul if and when I take my last breath."

Laney was openly crying. Skye made her way over to her, behind the sectional. She wrapped her arms around Laney as if she was the one who needed to feel safe and reassured. Afton watched them together.

"You're not alone," Afton spoke. "Stop acting as if you are." *Damn she was angry. At Skye for deceiving them. And especially at the unfairness of this hand that her little sister had been dealt at only forty years old. She had so much living left to do.*

"You have Knox. Laney has Brad and their boys. I have Bella. If I die, that immediate family of hers is no more. It's gone because I'm gone. This baby on the way will give Bella a family."

"What about this baby's father? You didn't give Knox the choice. Co-parenting was the plan." All Afton implied was that Knox had a right to know. She wouldn't purposely be hurtful and say that she felt like Skye manipulated him. And her, as well, because they shared their lives together.

"I don't want to fight with you about this," Skye stated in an effort to avoid the subject of Knox. Laney eyed both of her sisters. *This baby was already coming between them.*

"I don't either." Instead, she would talk to Knox later. Afton could only imagine what he was feeling. "Just do me a favor, both of us," Afton said to Skye as she also glanced at Laney. "Don't shut us out. We want to be there for you. One step at a time, together. Do you hear me?"

"I'd like that," Skye admitted. Suddenly she had dropped her armor. And that's when Afton reacted. She grabbed her, pulled her close and tight to her body. Afton probably should have been gentler and less aggressive. But there was an intensity now in the way she wanted to hold on for as long as she possibly could.

Chapter 22

Knox returned to the house with Bella. Afton saw them playing in the front yard, so she opened the door. When Bella saw her, she clearly uttered two words. "Come inside?" Afton stepped off the front porch and stood barefoot in the grass as she scooped up her sister's child in her arms. "Absolutely. Let's go see mommy."

Knox followed them inside. Afton didn't want to rush off her sisters, but she wanted the private time with him to talk about this sudden, heartbreaking change in their lives.

Bella was preoccupied once Knox joined them. He wanted to ask if everything was out in the open, but he didn't have to. He could clearly see their red eyes and tear-stained faces. He and Afton shared a sweet glance. She wanted to fall into his arms and find solace from this heartbreaking news. Then she watched him look over at Skye as she was the first to speak. "Thank you for helping with Bella."

"Anytime," he smiled softly. It wasn't as if Afton did not let it cross her mind before, but it certainly had now. *Bella would need a home too. One day. Eventually. God, she hoped that would be years away, if it had to happen at all.*

"My oncologist's office is on the grounds of Regency Memorial," Skye began to explain to her sisters. "Knox bumped into me as I was leaving an appointment." Afton imagined his confusion... and then shock. *Had he reacted as she did? Initially feeling manipulated? Or did he comfort her?* He obviously convinced Skye to no longer keep her illness a secret. "Telling my sisters was the right thing to do." She smiled sincerely at him, and Afton watched as he reached his hand to her. Skye, in turn, took his and briefly squeezed it. It was the first time Afton had ever seen them touch. They had always respectively kept their distance from each other. Afton had not been oblivious to that fact. Because of what happened between them, they never wanted Afton to question their loyalty to her once they gained back her trust. But that physical contact right now unnerved Afton. It shouldn't have. *She needed to get a grip. Be an adult. Knox had been there for her sister. She needed him. Skye was going to need all of them now.*

"I don't even know what to say," Knox spoke to Afton in their living room as the sun began to set and Afton attempted to close all of the window blinds on the main floor. Everyone had gone home now. She turned back to him. He was sitting on the arm of one end of the sectional. He still wore his dress clothes from the workday. He never had the chance to change, not even for the walk outside with Bella. She watched him run his fingers through his already disheveled brown hair.

Afton understood how Knox was feeling. "Can I ask you something?" He nodded. "Are you at all angry with Skye?"

"How can I be? This isn't her fault," Knox immediately defended Skye.

"I know that." *But what about the vital information that she kept from all of them?* "Skye knew she was sick before the IVF took place. She didn't have to go through with it. She had time to back out, or at least to tell us, and give us the chance to rethink this with a different light shed on it."

"I did have all of those same thoughts, but the thing is, nothing changed for Skye in terms of wanting to do this is for Bella. In fact, knowing she has a terminal illness enhanced her reasoning to do this. How could I dispute that?"

"That unborn baby is also yours." That was her answer.

"And mine alone if something happens to Skye..." his words were softly spoken and he looked down at floor. It was dark in that room, and neither one of them made any attempt to turn on a lamp.

"Does that scare you at all?"

"Some. Yes," he admitted, "because that wasn't our plan. But I think anyone who has lived a little knows that nothing ever goes by a blueprint. I keep reminding myself of this miracle. The fact that I am finally going to be a father. That's going to mean sacrifice and unconditional love. I want that. I've always been ready to give a little person, who will be a part of me, everything that I have."

Afton smiled, but that smile never met her eyes.

"Skye is lucky to have you."

"She has all of us," Knox reminded her.

Afton nodded in agreement. She wished she was able to say more, but she feared if she spoke at length, Knox would know how she really felt as she reeled from this truth. Knox instantly picked up on her uneasiness.

"Just tell me, Afton. What's weighing on your heart right now?"

She paused awhile before answering him. "My sister could die." She closed her eyes momentarily. "She could leave behind Bella and a baby. Your baby. Our lives were going to change regardless. I was prepared for that. I want you to have what you've dreamed of. But I'm imagining being full-time parents to a baby..." and no one had mentioned this yet, "and to Bella. They will be a package deal. So you asked what is weighing on my heart? I have feelings that I wish I could make go away. There's fear. Dread. Insecurity. I raised my children. I am going to have a grandchild before your baby with Skye is born." *Could she really start all over, raising children? She would be near seventy years old before they were young adults, out on their own.*

Knox sensed something was wrong because so much had changed, learning that Skye was ill. But he never expected Afton to have a complete change of heart. *How many times had he asked her if she was absolutely sure that she could be with him if he had a child? It was her initial idea!*

"I don't believe what I am hearing. So, in your mind, co-parenting was okay. Part-time sounded doable. But the possibility of full-time does not? I am going to be there for my child all of the time, no matter what the circumstances bring!" Knox raised his voice at her. This was their first official fight. This wasn't a little spat, or a measly argument. This was a hurtful, anger-fueled fight. "And I will also be there for Bella. I love that little girl like my own. You should too...she's your niece."

"Don't tell me how I should feel," Afton reacted. "I do love her. She's a part of my sister for God's sake. I spoil her and I bond with her, but she eventually goes home to her mother. I don't want to play that role."

"And do you think Skye wants to be sick and face the fact that she could die and be forced to leave her children behind? Can't you give her the peace of mind that they are going to be okay? Well taken care of and loved."

"Has Skye already asked this of you?"

"What? No." It was unspoken but understood. Knox knew that. Skye was counting on that.

"She's going to fight this and be in remission for a long time. From what she explained, she's already there." Even if it was false hope, Afton would hold onto it.

"I hope you're right," Knox told her.

"You're disappointed in me," Afton spoke quietly.

"Yeah, I am," he nearly spat back at her.

"We've always been honest with each other." Afton didn't know what else to say to him.

"Right," he stated, not looking at her this time.

The two of them had dinner plans tonight. Knox had told her to get dressed up and be ready to be wined and dined, and then made love to until the sun came up. That special evening had not happened for them. Afton never even made an attempt to get herself ready when their plans changed, because Skye needed them. It was okay, they both initially thought. They could reschedule a date for another time. Knox fingered the small black velvet box inside his front pant pocket while they shared silence in the dark living room. He physically ached from the disappointment. He wished for there to be another chance for him to ask Afton to be his wife. But, right now, they suddenly felt too far away from committing the rest of their lives to each other.

Chapter 23

The following morning, Afton stood in the kitchen in her favorite terrycloth robe. She sipped her coffee. It was a solemn moment of déjà vu for her. She felt alone and empty. She had not been in that place in a very long time. That was her old life with Sam. How could she allow that kind of distance to happen with Knox? This was her awakening. She was consumed with remorse. She didn't have a right to turn on him the way she did last night. It was hurtful and it was wrong. She could lose her sister. Bella and the baby on the way deserved to be loved and nurtured. She owed Knox an apology.

He walked in the kitchen, wearing only his navy-blue pajama bottoms that sat low on his waist. His sun-kissed, fit chest was bare. She stared. *God, that man. Her man. She was a foolish woman to push him away.*

"Morning," he spoke first. He didn't say *good*, because it didn't feel good to wake up beside her and not be able to share her space and hold her. There was too much hurt between them still.

"Knox... I'm sorry," Afton heard her voice crack. "You must think I am the most insensitive woman in the world. I didn't mean it. It was a reaction of fear. I'm afraid to lose my sister. I'm suddenly scared to death of a lot of things." *That was no excuse though. If she could take back her words last night, she would. Yes, she still had those uncertainties. But couldn't they face those together?*

He looked at her. She stood there in her robe. Her short-cropped hairstyle was rumpled from tossing and turning in her sleep last night as she was restless, and he had been too. He felt abandoned by her, just as he had by his ex-wife when she left him from the strain of their inability to conceive a child. He never believed Afton would make him feel as disappointed and lost and alone. But she had.

"I don't think you're insensitive," he began. "I felt letdown and hurt last night. I don't want to be in this alone. I need you in my life. I want you to be all-in this with me. We can power through anything, I know we can, as long as we are together. If that sounds corny, I get it, but it's how I feel. That's how *you* make me feel."

Afton took a few steps toward him. She reached for his face with both of her hands. The overnight stubble scratched her fingertips. He held her at the waist. He traced his fingers on the thick terrycloth material of the belt on her robe.

"I am all-in," she said to him, and he smiled before he kissed her hard and full on the mouth. The taste of coffee and toothpaste collided on their tongues. He reached down and opened her robe. She wore only panties underneath. His eyes on her body sometimes made her wish she didn't have the figure of a fifty-year-old. But the desire in his eyes, only for her, as she was, made her forget all about those insecurities on a body that was thicker than it once was.

"Make-up sex?" he asked her. She giggled. And clearly, she was *all-in* when her robe fell to the kitchen floor.

Laney poured orange juice into her Yeti, and then she added more than a splash of Tito's Handmade Vodka before she twisted and sealed the lid. She was going to school this morning to work in her classroom. In twelve days, the new school year would start. What a heartbreaking summer it had been for her family. First, Liam. And now, Skye.

Brad made his way into the kitchen before Laney left. "You okay?" he asked her.

"I'm not sure if I'll ever be okay if we lose her," she admitted.

"Lane. You said so yourself how people can live decades with this, in remission or with consistent medication. Remember, we promised ourselves to stay positive when Liam was diagnosed. Keep that mindset for Skye, too. I will help you in any way I can, you know that." Brad was worried about Laney turning to alcohol even more. She was dependent on it now.

"Keep reminding me of that when I need it, okay?" He kissed her lightly on the lips.

"I need breakfast," he stated.

"And I have to go. I want to finish getting my classroom ready so I can relax for the remaining days of summer. She made a sad face and groaned about having to get back into a structured routine. "Where did I leave my car keys?" she glanced at the counter and then left the kitchen to search further. Brad stood near the table. He looked down at her Yeti cup next to her handbag. He lifted the cup to his nose. *Orange juice?* He tipped it to his mouth. The vodka was potent on his tongue. He swallowed and instantly his eyes burned. His face fell. *As if he didn't already know... his wife was an alcoholic.*

Skye, on the end of the exam table, faced Dr. Fruend who straddled his stool. This had become the norm for them to meet every few weeks to discuss the results of yet another blood draw. Dylan Fruend held his breath each time the lab report made its way back to him. He prayed for her, for no drastic changes. She was successfully living with this disease, as there had yet to be any signs or symptoms in these early stages. But as the disease progressed, there could be bone destruction, anemia (a lack of red blood cells) or even kidney failure. He was honest and upfront with Skye at every consultation. He answered her questions, sparing no detail to save her from panic or worry. And then he always reminded her that she was far from being entirely affected by this disease. Say it for me, he would tell her. *I am in remission.* She repeated those words and smiled at him in return.

"No change," he grinned, and his entire face was lit. She saw so much skin when she looked at that man. A clean-shaven face, and not a hair on his head. His eyebrows were dark and his eyes were the bluest she had ever looked into. Well she hadn't actually looked into them, but from a distance on the end of the exam table, she saw the sincerity in his eyes every time he spoke to her about her health. *He wanted to save her life. He never said those words out loud. But, by the grace of God, he did.*

"Oh, thank you," Skye let out a serious sigh of relief.

"Don't thank me. I'm only the messenger."

"You are more than that, and you know it." She complimented him, and he felt a wave of something invigorating wash over him.

"Keep doing what you're doing. Eat well, rest plenty," he began. "I realize you have a little one to put first, but you are doing a great job taking care of yourself. I'm sure once the baby arrives, rest will be a challenge for you. Maybe consider outside help?"

"I definitely will." She was counting on Knox, and certainly knew she could. And for what it was worth, she felt like saying as much right now. "The baby's father will be thoroughly involved."

He raised an eyebrow. She was single, had a surrogate carrying her baby, and Dylan Fruend assumed there was a sperm donor. How else did single mothers accomplish that? He was about to find out. "I don't follow. So there was a father involved in the IVF process?"

Skye nodded her head. "I sort of feel like I want to share this with you. Other than my family, I don't go around giving out the details of my personal life." But he was more than her doctor. He was clearly becoming a trusted friend. She had his undivided attention. "My oldest sister's life began again at fifty. She was in a loveless marriage, and then she met her soul mate. I will spare you all the details, but this man she's committed to now has never been a dad. My sister has two adult children and is beyond her reproductive years and cannot give him any children. But she wanted to give him the gift of having a child of his own." She refrained from adding that she and her sisters had witnessed his gift with children, with Bella especially. Skye had never trusted a man more. They shared a connection, and it ran deeper than succumbing to a sexual encounter one night. It wasn't a passion-driven or infatuation kind of love, but Skye cared very deeply for Knox Manning.

Dylan Fruend's eyes widened. It wasn't difficult to piece together what Skye was explaining. "Your sister's new love is the father of your baby?"

"Yes. Crazy, I know. But we will co-parent and give our baby the best of both of our worlds, just separately. And now that I know I'm sick," Skye paused, "he will be able to raise our child if I can't."

He brushed off her last comment. That wasn't going to happen. Not on his watch. "I've heard a lot of out of the ordinary things in my years of practice, but this just might top the list," he smiled. "I am not judging any of you, really. In fact, what I've taken away from this amazing plan in progress is you all are a bunch of selfless compassionate people. I'm honored to know you, Skye Gallant." *If only he could get to know her better.*

"You don't think I've lost my mind?"

"Not at all." he smiled. And she suppressed a giggle.

"What about you? Any children of your own?" She noticed long before now that he did not wear a wedding band.

"None that I know of!" he joked, and then he laughed as loud as Skye did.

Skye watched him roll back his stool and steady it under the table in the corner. She had been sharing space with him in this setting long enough now to know that was how he wrapped up their scheduled time. Skye was a little taken aback by how regretful she was that their time was up. She enjoyed being with him, more than she realized before. Skye started to move off the end of the exam table, and he reached for her hand to assist her. That's all it was. Just help down from a higher surface. But his touch lingered long after he let go. She ached for more. She chided herself. *He was her doctor!* And then she diagnosed herself as just lonely. It had been a long time since she connected with a man. Not since Knox Manning.

Chapter 24

Seven months later...

Knox paced the length of the waiting room at Regency Memorial. Skye was bookended by her sisters on the chairs against the wall. "He's going to wear out the flooring," Laney noted, and took a sip of the bottled water she brought from home in her handbag.

After almost twelve hours of labor, Savannah was being prepped for an emergency cesarean section. They all felt terrible for her. She would have a longer recovery and a permanent scar from a baby that wasn't hers. Laney was the last one to be with her before she was carted off on a gurney. "I just want this over," she had cried. Laney held her and reminded her to be strong, and she would have her life back very soon. Being a gestational surrogate was an incredible sacrifice.

This unplanned turn of events had rattled everyone. Especially Savannah. In haste, she requested that no one be in the operating room with her. The complications, combined with everyone in the delivery room, had completely overwhelmed her. The nurse shared that news with Skye and Knox just moments ago. They were both upset and truly disappointed not to witness the second their baby was born, but they would be there for the first moments right after. That's what Savannah wanted, and she had just gone through hell in the delivery room for them. But to no avail. The baby had not been born naturally.

"I think someone should be in there with her," Knox pointed out again. "What about you, Laney? You're the closest to her."

"You heard the nurse. She wants to be alone." Laney emptied her water bottle and Afton noticed she put it back in her handbag.

"Let's just respect Savannah's wishes and hope and pray this will all be over for her and the rest of us very soon," Skye stated. She wanted so badly to see her baby and hold him or her. The gender was going to be a surprise for them.

"Let's all do a gender vote again!" Afton suggested, trying to lighten the mood in there.

"We've done this how many times now?" Skye asked her. "The majority vote is a boy."

"And you won't tell any of us what names you have picked out!" Laney rolled her eyes. Knox chuckled. He didn't know the names either. That was something he wanted to leave up to Skye. He didn't care if they weren't a typical family, doing things the standard way. *Did that really matter? That baby, his baby, was going to be so loved by everyone.* He waited years for this moment. And now it was here.

Afton and Laney entered the operating room with the intention to stay back at first. This moment was going to be for Skye and Knox. Savannah was awake, as she had been given spinal epidural anesthesia for the cesarean birth, and the doctor was stitching her incision now. They were told to remain on the opposite side of the curtain. They heard the baby's cries as one of the nurses hovered over the newborn on the scale.

"Don't tell us, don't say anything, we want to see for ourselves!" Skye preached in her typical loud matter, as she made her way across the room with Knox following close behind. She didn't want anyone to ruin the gender surprise. Afton wanted to calmly remind her to be respectful in that environment, as the medical staff was still present, but she refrained. *This was her little sister's moment. Who cared if she was loud and disruptive?*

The nurse giggled as she lifted the unclothed baby into the air and Skye covered her mouth with both of her hands. It was a girl.

Another baby girl! Bella would grow up with a sister.

She immediately cradled her. Her scrunched up little round face was the most beautiful thing she had ever seen. Just like when Bella was born. *She had two girls!* Skye silently thanked God at that moment for allowing her to be there, to be alive. The cancer in her blood continued to stay in remission. *She was blessed.*

It was as if time stood still. Knox stood beside Skye. He gently touched those tiny little fingers. "She's so beautiful..." Skye said to him. "Do you want to hold your baby girl?" There were tears streaming down his face. He nodded, because that's all he could muster at this point. Afton and Laney stood in a close circle with them, choking on their sobs. *This was a miracle.*

She had a lot of thick, light brown hair, and Afton smiled when she noticed how wavy it already looked. *Like her daddy's.* She was elated for Knox right now. Like a movie on the big screen, she watched these moments play out in front of her. *Skye was a mother again to another precious girl. Bella would have her lifetime sidekick to count on. And Knox, the man she adored and would absolutely do anything for, was finally a father.* Afton would remember this moment forever. Yes, she had a hand in bringing them to this point. But so much else had fallen into place as well. She didn't want to take credit. She only wanted to be a part of it.

Knox was so careful with how he handled her. She opened her eyes when he spoke to her. "Hello baby girl... I'm your daddy." This was an unconditional, wear your heart outside of your body, kind of love. Afton was right...there was not a thing on this earth like the feeling he had right now. His heart was full.

He looked at Afton now. She was watching him closely. She smiled wide with tears clouding her eyes again. "Come closer to see her," he said. "She looks like a Gallant girl." They all laughed.

"What else are we going to call her?" Laney asked. They had waited long enough to find out her name.

"Blair Hope Manning."

Her sisters gasped. Her name triggered more tears. "Blair means field of battle. She's going to help me with my fight to live for a very long time. And Hope," Skye looked at Knox, "was our mother's name."

"It's perfect, just like her."

Spoken like a proud daddy.

Blair Hope Manning. *She had his name. She was a part of him and would be forever.* Knox was completely taken with his baby in his arms.

Chapter 25

Laney had gone behind the curtain to hold her friend's hand. Savannah was consumed with emotion when she saw her. She was spent from an unsuccessful labor, remorseful for pushing everyone away, and relieved the baby was finally born safe and sound.

"No need to apologize," Laney shushed her. "You were wonderful for the last nine months. We all have a right to shut down at some point."

Savannah smiled just as the curtain was pulled back and the rest of them joined Laney at her bedside. Knox was holding the baby, but he got close to Savannah so he could bend down and kiss her on the forehead. "We are forever grateful," he told her. "Thank you for everything."

"Told you," Laney winked at her. "Everything is fine."

Savannah's mother was going to stay with her at the hospital for the next day or so, until she was released. And now, Laney and Afton were waiting for Skye and Knox to finalize the paperwork so they could bring their baby home. Baby Blair was going to spend the first month of her life getting settled into a routine with Skye and her big sister Bella. Knox could visit day or night, Skye told him, and they all knew he would. The nursery, in all neutral colors, was also ready for the baby at Knox and Afton's house on Holly Avenue. Once she was a few weeks old, they would keep her with them on a rotating basis with Skye. They all agreed it was important for Bella to be with her baby sister often, so it was a given that she would also be packing for many sleepovers.

"This is going to get harder," Laney spoke with her voice low, "this plan to shuffle Blair back and forth."

"Don't you think I know that?" Afton reacted. "But life is hard. We all have something that weighs us down. You already know this. For the love of God, Skye has cancer. Your boy has a serious lung condition. And you can't seem to function without drinking." Laney's eyes widened. She stayed silent. "Don't think it's not obvious. You are dependent on alcohol. Who totes around their own water bottle that smells like blueberry vodka?"

"Don't say anything to anyone else, please," Laney spoke in almost a whisper.

"Promise me you will get it under control, Lane."

"I can handle it, I swear."

Afton didn't believe her. Addiction was a destructive path. It always put its victims on a downward spiral into a deep dark hole. And not everyone could survive the fight to climb back up.

Skye had done the single mother thing before. It was not difficult for her, nor had it taken any adjustment for her to grasp the concept of parenting two babies alone. Bella had even been more accepting of the newest addition to their family than Skye had anticipated. Having Knox present and a part of their little family was refreshing for Skye. He soaked up the newness of parenthood, he learned all that he could about being a first-time parent, and he simply was the most doting and loving daddy to his baby. Knox also included Bella in everything they did together. She had to be ready with a diaper when Knox changed the baby. She had to find the pacifier, the one that her baby sister had already gotten attached to and needed when she was fussy. This arrangement brought Skye happiness. Until her baby turned four weeks old, and it was time she was introduced to her other home on Holly Avenue with her daddy and Afton.

Knox was more than ready to begin the next phase of parenting. He had yet to spend an entire night under the same roof with Blair. He stayed late at Skye's house many nights, but he never slept there. Some of those times Afton had been with him, but not all of those nights. And out of respect for her, he never stayed all night long. He didn't conceal the fact that he missed his baby endlessly when he wasn't with her. Afton understood, and reminded him that would change soon.

Bella was also invited to spend a few nights with Baby Blair at Knox and Afton's house. Skye was touched by their kindness. If her girls were going to grow up close, they needed to be together full-time, not just once in awhile.

Being alone in her house was too much for Skye to handle. She had the opportunity to do anything she wanted, to go anywhere, and she was at home. She would get a full, uninterrupted night of sleep. That appealed to her. She still felt healthy and strong, and for that she was very thankful.

Skye held her phone in her hand. She could send just one text to check on her girls. She could ask Afton to send her pictures. Or she could leave them be and find something to do. For herself. For her sanity.

The woman she used to be would go to a bar, strike up conversations, flirt, and maybe gain the attention of a male companion by the end of the night. That wasn't her life anymore. At least it had not been for quite awhile. But she thought about how she suddenly felt free again. Her body missed the physical contact. Everyone's life lacked something. A man by her side, for better or worse, was not meant to be for her. There were so many reasons why it would never be. She was a single mom — and she was also sick. The cancer inside of her body wasn't going to behave itself forever.

Skye forced herself to stop wallowing, and she left the house.

She drove around in her jeep for almost an hour, and finally she parked it on her sister's driveway. If she couldn't bother one sister tonight, she would visit the other. Laney wasn't home though, and after Skye rang the doorbell twice, she relented and walked back to her jeep. The neighborhood where Laney and Brad raised their boys was always busy. People were active and outside in their yards, walking on the sidewalks, or chatting alongside the street. It was inviting. Everyone seemed to enjoy each other. Skye, wearing a pair of comfortable running shorts, a tank top, and tennis shoes, decided to take a walk out there. It would be good to clear her head. Or, if anything, preoccupy her mind for a little while. She locked her cell phone and her handbag in her jeep and took off walking.

She was at least two miles from Laney's house by now. She was alone on a sidewalk. No other walkers or bikers were around at the moment. Only up ahead, there was a man washing his car at the end of his driveway. Skye contemplated stepping out on the road before she got closer. The power washer he was using was spraying well over the sidewalk and onto the road. Skye would be in that wet path if she didn't move off the sidewalk. She stepped closer, but before she veered off her path and onto the street, she recognized him.

She had never seen him wear a pair of shorts before. He had flip flops on those feet that were always in socks and shoes, typically dress shoes. His hairless head was sun-kissed. His red t-shirt hugged him in all the right places. Those broad shoulders, thick chest, and tight abs. He saw her as well. He stopped what he was doing and met her on the suds-filled curb behind his black sedan.

"Skye?" She smiled. It felt strange to see him out of his element. He had a life. A house. A car. He wore play clothes and sandals. He was a human being who just happened to be a medical genius. Skye had previously heard all the success stories. He was a phenomenal physician. She believed every positive word about him now.

"Dr. Fruend, hi! So, this is where you live?" It was a two-story, brick home that looked like it housed at least four bedrooms. Skye understood wanting to live in a big house, even it if was too much space for just one person. She chose to do the same thing, before she brought Bella into her life. And now Blair.

"Yes. Do you approve?" he teased her.

"It's a beautiful home," she smiled, "but that's not what I meant. I wasn't judging your taste. I'm just surprised to see you, that's all. My sister and her family live nearby, probably two miles. I parked and walked from there."

He nodded. "All alone tonight?"

She let out a nervous laugh. "Uh, yes. It's a rarity for me, but I have some me time to enjoy."

"Good for you." One leg of his long khaki cargo shorts was damp. His feet were drenched in those flip-flops and they squeaked when he stepped. "So does your sister have the girls?" *He remembered that she had another baby girl.*

"Yes, and no," Skye began. "I have two sisters. Laney, who lives near here, was not home when I got there awhile ago. My other sister, Afton, is keeping my girls tonight. She and the man she lives with are—"

"He's your baby's father, right?" Of course he remembered that story.

"Yes. Thanks for saving me that explanation again!" she laughed out loud.

He smiled. "How's everything working out with that arrangement?" Yes, it was a personal question, but Skye didn't mind.

"So far, it's wonderful. I mean, this is my first night alone. And I already don't like being in an empty house without my babies… but I will get into a routine for myself. It will be good for everyone."

"I'm sure it will."

"Can I ask you something, Dr. Freund?"

"Only if you call me Dylan."

Skye's eyes widened.

"Please, we are out of the office. It's fine."

"Okay. Dylan." She liked the way his name felt on her tongue and sounded inside her head when she spoke it. "Do you live alone? Girlfriend? Partner?"

He laughed. "No partner. I'm straight…" but he appreciated how worldly she was, "and my ex-girlfriend moved out about six months ago."

"Oh," Skye made a regretful face, as if she should not have pried or opened up an old wound.

"No, it's fine. Not meant to be."

"Right," Skye agreed.

"My turn?" he asked.

"For what?"

"To ask you a question."

Skye giggled. "Sure, ask away. Ask me anything." He already knew her life hadn't landed on the standard path. She had nothing to hide.

"How do you feel about pizza, say, loaded with all the toppings and extra cheese? Delivered to my back patio?"

His invitation caught her by surprise. Her doctor just asked her out. Well, technically not *out*, but a pizza date in his backyard was close enough. "Does anyone ever turn down pizza?" she teased him.

"Is that a yes, by chance?"

"Yes, Dylan. I would love to."

Chapter 26

"Where's Skye?" Laney asked her family as she came through her front door and didn't see her in the living room with her boys and Brad, who were all immersed in playing a game of Fortnite.

"We thought she was with you," Luke answered.

"Her jeep was here when we got home," Brad added.

"Really?" Laney dug in her handbag for her phone, and immediately dialed. Her call to Skye went to voicemail. "Well, where is she? Tonight is the first night for Knox and Afton to have the baby and Bella too." Her initial thought, when she saw Skye's jeep on her driveway, had been she must have needed to get out of the quiet house. Laney still believed this custody back-and-forth arrangement was going to be difficult for everyone.

"Maybe she went for a walk?" Brad suggested.

"Yeah," Laney thought that too. "I want to go look for her. It's going to be dark soon."

"She's a big girl, Lane," Brad commented.

"I know that, but what if she got sick or something?" None of them should take for granted that Skye was going to stay in remission.

"Right, I'm sorry, I wasn't thinking. Let's take a drive around and look for her."

Laney rushed out the front door of their house with Brad on her heels.

Skye sat back on the cushioned wrought iron chair underneath Dylan's covered patio. "I'm stuffed," she commented patting her belly that still looked incredibly fit and flat underneath the elastic of her shorts. She had eaten three pieces of pizza and was sipping a glass of red wine.

"It's good to see firsthand that your appetite is going strong," Dylan stated, as he sat on a chair adjacent to hers.

"Hey, we agreed, no doctor-patient talk," she reminded him.

"Right... but as your friend, it's good to see that you can almost out-eat me with pizzas slices." He had also eaten three.

"I don't skimp when I eat," she informed him. "I just work out like a crazy person to show those calories who's boss."

He chuckled. "Take it easy on yourself. You would be equally as beautiful if you were chubby."

This time Skye laughed out loud. "Can't say a man has ever said that to me before." This man was looking out for her health. Any extra weight would benefit her if she ever had to begin treatment for the myeloma. Skye realized what he was thinking, but she chose to keep their conversation light. This had been a wonderful evening with him.

He looked in her eyes and smiled at her. She felt his hand cover hers on the table. She opened her palm and intertwined her fingers with his. A welcomed sensation warmed her body. "I care about you, Skye Gallant."

"I could get used to this, seeing you outside of your office, I mean."

He thought about how to say what he needed to say to her. "I don't want to be your doctor forever. What I mean is, I will monitor your case day in and day out... but eventually I will not be able to see you as a patient."

"Are you asking me to find a different oncologist, because I don't want to. I need you! You're the best there is. You're it for me. You've kept me healthy!" This thought was so upsetting for her. She let go of his hand.

"Wait. No. Slow down. All I'm saying is... I may have to assign a colleague to your case, if you were to ever agree to date me."

Date him? He had just gone from firing her as his patient to wanting to get closer to her. "I'm not ready to lose you as my doctor... but I could see us enjoying getting to know each other better."

"Good," he winked at her. "Nothing has to be decided right now. One moment at a time, okay?"

She touched his hand again. The sun was beginning to set. She knew she had to get going. If she hadn't left her car parked at Laney's, and her cell phone inside, she wouldn't be concerned with ending their time together. "I really need to get back to my sister's house soon."

"I understand. Let me drive you. It's too far to walk alone in the dark."

She appreciated his concern. "I'd like that, thank you."

But first, he wanted to kiss her. And she hoped he would.

Skye watched him lean toward her, over the tabletop. He touched her cheek with his open palm and moved his lips toward hers. It was gentle. Almost soothing. Like melting butter in her mouth. Their tongues touched. Their kiss deepened. And when it was over, she was breathless. And what he said next, confirmed their connection. "I've been wanting to do that since the first time I saw you."

She initiated another passionate kiss, and this time there was an urgency between them. *If she hadn't abandoned her damn jeep tonight, she would let this man take her bed. Or in the grass in his backyard.*

The moment Laney and Brad returned home from their drive around their neighborhood and its outskirts, Laney had her phone in hand. "I'm calling the police. Skye seriously is missing!"

"I would wait on that if I were you," Brad told her, as he looked into his rearview mirror. Laney whipped her head around. A car drove off as Skye was walking up the driveway. Laney jumped out of the car in the garage and ran to her.

"Where in the hell have you been?"

Skye held both of her hands up in the space between them. "Calm down. I know I should not have left my car here, with my phone in it. I only intended to go for a short walk once I discovered you weren't home."

"You were walking this whole time?"

"No. I was about two miles away, in a subdivision, when I found my doctor's house. He was actually outside washing his car."

"Your doctor?" The only male doctor of Skye's that Laney knew of was her oncologist. She knew he had an amazing reputation, and was in his forties, but that was all.

"Dylan Fruend."

"Dylan?" Laney frowned.

"We talk during my appointments, I mean really talk to each other. I've felt a subtle connection to him, but I never read into anything. I just assumed I was reacting out of gratitude."

"And now what changed? Oh sweet Jesus. You slept with him, didn't you! That's why your cheeks are all flushed."

Skye giggled. "No, I did not sleep with him. He invited me for pizza and wine under his covered patio."

"So just a friendly dinner?"

"Until we kissed. Oh God can that man kiss…"

Laney rolled her eyes. "You know you can't make out with your doctor. He could lose his license for chrissakes."

"He mentioned what might have to change once we start seeing each other…"

"You're dating him now?"

"Yeah… and it's been a long time since I wanted to get to know a man."

Laney's frustration suddenly dissipated. "Awe honey. Are you falling for him?"

"All I know for sure is there's so much uncertainty about my future. My girls are my whole world. But a part of me suddenly wants to take this chance and make room in my heart for potential true love." It may not be lasting love, but Skye wanted to relish the experience of it for as long as it lasted.

Chapter 27

By the third week of having the baby —and often Bella— live with them part-time, Knox and Afton had fallen into a routine. They were exhausted at times, but happy. Knox was so in love with fatherhood, and his baby girl. Afton's heart overflowed with gratitude whenever she watched them together. No matter how much a baby had altered (and yes, disrupted) their lives, Afton recognized this much-deserved blessing for Knox. Yes, she missed when it was just the two of them with no added responsibilities. But Afton tried very hard not let their new life overwhelm her. She made a point to give Knox his space with Baby Blair too. That's when she periodically left the house and made her way over to her daughter, Amy's apartment to see her grandson. Grey Samuel was born two months before Blair, and Afton was a proud granny to her first grandchild. Children had filled her life with joy again, and it was an unexpected bliss for Afton. They made her feel young again. *Except when she was sleep deprived.* Lack of sleep felt a hell of a lot different when she was twenty years younger.

Skye and Dylan had eased into this dating thing. The week following their impromptu pizza date on his patio, he invited her over to his house again. That time, he cooked for her. He swore he wasn't of Italian descent, but the pasta he prepared for them was the best Skye ever tasted. Two more dates, both at fine-dining restaurants in the Twin Cities, followed. They were getting closer. Their conversations always brought them to a deeper level when they shared their truest feelings. Dylan knew her hopes and her fears. And Skye knew of him as the most compassionate man she had ever met, but he fiercely guarded his heart. That caution stemmed from previous heartbreaks. Each date ended with passionate kissing. But they had not gone to bed together. There was something special about taking things slow, getting to know each other, and waiting to have sex. And then there was the other end of it. *Skye lived in the moment now more than ever. And Dylan lived like they had all the time in the world to be together.*

Laney had fallen back into the routine of teaching eighth grade science. Luckily, there were two teachers for each subject in every grade level. Otherwise, Laney would be teaching her own sons this school year. Luke would have just gone along with it. Liam, however, would have been challenging. He continued to be her defiant son. He did honor his word and he gave up vaping to preserve his damaged lungs. His interest in girls was another story. He was spending almost all of his free time with Shey, the sixteen-year-old neighbor girl. The night before last, he missed his 9:30 curfew on a Saturday night. Laney had been waiting for him when he came home more than an hour late. She was angry and when she attempted to punish him for being late, and for ignoring her two texts and one call, he called her out on her drinking. *She wasn't drunk*, she told him. And his response stayed with her, "*Maybe not, mom. But always having to be semi-sober isn't a way to live either. We see it. Dad hates it. You need to give up alcohol just like I had to quit vaping.*"

It had been five weeks since the Gallant girls made time for each other. No excuses were made, their lives had just gotten more complex. There was the baby. And Dylan Fruend. And Laney didn't need another reason to drink. Both Skye and Afton were worried about her. Yet here they were, in Laney's kitchen, and she had just poured the Moscato.

Afton and Skye shared a glance in each other's direction when Laney took a long sip from her glass and then topped it off again before setting aside the bottle. *At least she wasn't trying to hide it anymore.*

"So, who's first?" Laney asked, ignoring their disapproving looks. Judgment from anyone wasn't that difficult for her to disregard anymore.

"I could brag all night long about Blair Hope," Skye smiled wide.

"She is a doll," Afton agreed.

"How's Knox doing with her?" Laney asked. "Have the 2 a.m. feedings gotten to him yet?" They giggled.

"He's very good about everything, including the lack of sleep." Afton stated. It was odd that Afton was answering questions about Skye's baby's daddy. It was almost as if Skye felt unnerved. She wanted to add her opinion of Knox as well. *She was beyond impressed too.*

"He's amazing with her. She knows his voice. She smiles in response. Her little legs and arms are kicking and flailing when she first sees him. I obviously lacked a partner in this when I had Bella, so I'm enjoying the co-parenting thing. I really couldn't imagine a man more wonderful to father my child." Skye boasted, and held nothing back.

She perhaps had gone too far with that comment. Afton creased her brow. She had her hand on her wine glass and she was going to just take a long swig and let her rebuttal settle somewhere between her appropriate and inappropriate thoughts. But, no, she spoke regardless. "What is that supposed to mean?" Afton spat at Skye. "There are other wonderful fathers out there. I'm sure you would offend Dylan Fruend with that comment."

"No. I mean yes. But I'm done having babies! We all know that." Skye was frazzled.

"Right. We do know that," Laney interrupted, in an effort to keep the peace between her sisters. This baby was definitely forcing them to be too close for comfort. "So how are you and Dylan doing? Still enjoying the getting-to-know-each-other phase?"

Skye smiled, and appeared to relax. "It's nice. It really is. It's simply refreshing to be with someone who understands me.

There are no false pretenses with him. It's like he knows my soul sometimes."

"You're in love," Afton softened, and smiled.

"I know I am, but we haven't said it yet. I know it's going to be a shock to you both, but we are taking things very slowly."

"Does that mean what I think it does?" Laney snickered. "No sex?" Skye sulked and nodded to confirm that. "Are you even our sister?"

It was true. Skye had been the most amorous of the three. She lost her virginity at the earliest age, at fifteen. She also outnumbered them with sexual partners. It wasn't a competition. It certainly wasn't something she boasted about. It had just been Skye's lifestyle for awhile. For a very long time, she didn't need a man for anything else.

"He really is taking this courting thing seriously. I'm touched by his gentleman nature, but steamy kisses leave me panting and unsatisfied." They giggled.

"I'm happy for you, you know that," Afton reminded her. They had already talked somewhat at length about *her budding relationship with her doctor* when shuffling the baby back and forth between their homes.

"Me too," Laney chimed in, while she finished off her first glass of Moscato.

"I can't explain it," Skye began. "I just never wanted a relationship. I wanted sex. It's not that I didn't pick and choose carefully." She was talking about Bella's father, but did not elaborate. Her high school sweetheart moved away after graduation. Skye of course knew his background, was assured that he had good genes. She seduced him at their 20th class reunion. After reuniting for just one night, they parted ways again. The biological father of Skye's firstborn daughter lived in California and was not aware of Bella because Skye had never told a soul. "I often found real connections," Skye attempted to explain, "I just didn't allow it to go farther than anything physical. But with Dylan, there's an intimacy between us, and we haven't even slept together. Maybe I could have had that with another man? I guess I just wasn't ready. Or, Dylan is finally the one."

Afton felt uncomfortable. All she could imagine was Skye flirting, connecting with, and falling for Knox. *Had she truly stopped herself from falling for Knox, or had she hidden those feelings? Having his baby certainly had bonded them.* Afton tried to steer her own destructive thoughts away from this nonsense. But she had spent weeks pushing down or shoving away some of these feelings. It got to her every single time Skye sent Knox a text message with a photo of Baby Blair attached, and Afton would occasionally intercept it. "*Someone misses the best daddy in the world,*" the last one had read. That was fine. It was sweet and endearing. If Skye would have left it at that. But then, she had to add phrases like, "*You really are amazing with her. We are so blessed to have you in our lives.*"

This was co-parenting, Afton reminded herself. That was all. Knox was wholeheartedly committed to her. And now Skye was falling for her doctor. Even still, with the wine in her system, Afton felt bolder and wished to speak her mind. Nothing was holding her back.

"Did you pick and choose carefully that night with Knox?" Afton began. "Was he one of your potential genuine connections?"

"Afton!" Laney interjected. "You can't be serious. Now? After all this time, you're doing this now?"

Skye straightened her posture at the table, directly across from Afton. "No, it's fine. I'll answer that. Knox isn't like most men. What woman wouldn't find him attractive and interesting? Yeah, I felt a strong connection to him. But he was already taken. His heart belonged to you — then and now."

"Stop trying to appease me," Afton stated, clearly annoyed, but still on some sort of unnecessary rampage.

"I'm not! You need to stop whining and appreciate what you have!"

"Are you implying that I do not appreciate Knox?"

"Girls!" Laney interjected as their mother did so very often. With three girls, there was drama and disagreements. But this wasn't some petty childhood argument. This was real life and Laney believed her sisters were dealing with a delicate subject that should simply be left alone. And perhaps it could have been if there wasn't a baby in the middle. "Stop hurting each other."

"You sound like mom," Skye noted. And Afton sighed.

"If mom were here, you two would break her heart with your hurtful words."

"Like your drinking habit wouldn't send her over the edge!" Afton spat as a matter of fact, but the jab was inappropriate. Skye's eyes widened. She easily had the same thought, but for once in her life she kept her mouth shut. She didn't have the energy for it. There was no point in fighting with both of her sisters. One was clearly enough. And she was tired tonight. She should have eaten dinner, as the wine was not sitting well in her stomach. She heard her sisters swapping words. Their voices sounded far away, and almost echoed at times in her head. And the last thing she remembered was slouching forward and everything went black.

Chapter 28

It was strange how waiting rooms in a medical setting could feel, depending on what was happening. When Afton, her sisters, and Knox all were waiting for the birth of Blair Hope, there was anticipation and excitement (combined with some apprehension). But, like now, when the situation felt urgent and dire, there was nothing but panic and fear racing through the minds of those left behind to wait. To hear the news. *What happened? Would the person they loved be okay?*

Among those awful emotions, Afton felt guilt. She never should have fought with Skye. She initiated it. It was solely her fault. Her sister was sick, even if it hadn't seemed like it for months on end while her blood levels remained status quo. Afton was ashamed of herself. Unjustifiable jealousy had raged inside her. Her emotions, all that stemmed from the past few weeks, simply boiled over and she lashed out at her youngest sister.

As We Are

Knox barged through the waiting room door. He had been on the grounds at a hospital board meeting to speak on behalf of the upcoming ball. He left the moment Afton called him, which was after she and Laney arrived at the hospital. He was concerned about the baby and Bella, and Afton reassured him they were asleep at Laney's house, where Brad and the boys were keeping a good eye on them. *Just hurry*, she had told him. *I'm really worried about Skye.* She had regained consciousness once the paramedics arrived. Both Afton and Laney followed behind the ambulance. Neither spoke a word.

"How is she?" Knox made his way over to the chair beside Afton.

"We don't know. We're still waiting to hear. We called Dylan, but I'm sure you already know that." He joined the ER doctor just moments ago. Both Knox and Dylan had gotten the same emergency call just as the board meeting adjourned. Laney had called Dylan from Skye's phone. Dylan was aware of the shared connection between Skye and Knox. Skye told him weeks ago that his colleague fathered her child via IVF and was in a serious relationship with her sister. Dylan thought highly of Knox and didn't judge. In fact, Skye had smiled at him (and perhaps fell in love with him a little more) when he mentioned something to the effect of... *small world, isn't it!*

"We were talking," Laney chose her words carefully, "while sitting at the kitchen table. And Skye suddenly caught us both off guard when she passed out. She didn't fall or hurt herself. She just slumped forward on the table."

Knox was silent for a moment. God, he hoped this wasn't the cancer rearing its ugly head. *Please no. Bella and Blair needed her. He needed her. She was the mother of his baby.* "Let's hope it's nothing serious...or related to the cancer," he spoke softly. "Dylan's got her. We have to trust that he can help her." *Save her. Prolong her life.* Afton reached for his hand.

It felt like too much time had passed. There was no word from anyone. Knox stood up to stretch his legs and asked both Afton and Laney if they wanted some water, or coffee or anything. Afton declined. Laney asked for a cup of coffee. And she didn't even drink coffee. Perhaps she wanted it to counteract the alcohol in her system. Afton stayed silent. Until Knox left the room.

"Are you feeling alright?" she asked Laney.

"Yeah, why? Are you going to prod at me too because you think I'm intoxicated?"

"Stop. Please. I feel terrible about all of it. I don't know what came over me."

"Well you should feel awful. Everything you said was uncalled for. Leave well enough alone for fuck's sake!"

Afton leaned forward and put her face in her hands. *Damn it. She hated to cry!*

As We Are

Knox was trying his best to keep the conversation going in the waiting room, but Afton and Laney were not feeling very much like talking. Finally, Dylan joined them.

The sisters instantly stood the moment they saw him. He was wearing his white lab coat overtop top a casual polo shirt and dark washed denim and boat shoes. He wasn't on call, but he put himself in charge of Skye's emergency. He was her oncologist and he wanted tests run tonight. *Stat.*

"How is she?" Afton blurted out first. Her nerves were wracked. She needed some answers now. Knox joined them in their huddle. He saw the worry in Dylan's eyes earlier when the two of them raced through the hospital corridors and took the elevator down to the ER. Knox could tell he truly cared about Skye. And right now, he too, was anxious to hear what was going on with her.

"This is an unexpected way to meet you both for the first time," Dylan referred to Skye's sisters, "but in any case, I'm Dylan Fruend."

"It's nice to meet you," Laney offered her hand, and Afton followed. They would save the pleasantries for another time. Dylan knew everyone was wondering about Skye and fretting about her health.

"We did some quick blood work," that explained their long wait, "and it appears that Skye is anemic." He watched her sisters begin to relax a little. "Anemia is a condition which occurs when there is deficiency of red blood cells, or there are dysfunctional red blood cells. It can lead to reduced oxygen flow to the body's organs. Among other things, it can cause fatigue, decreased energy, and lightheadedness."

"So that explains why she passed out?" Laney interjected.

"Yes. Most times, anemia is an iron deficiency and is treated with iron pills or vitamins. In Skye's case, however, her red blood cells are normal in size but low in number, and this is called normocytic anemia."

"How is that different? Is it more severe?" Knox asked, outright. It was interesting how both of them were doctors, but their specializations were vastly different.

"It's the type of anemia that accompanies chronic disease."

The cancer.

Myeloma.

Cancer of the blood.

All of their thoughts raced. For so long, Skye had been doing amazingly well. *Why couldn't that continue?*

"It is treatable. I want to start with iron pills and vitamins and see where that takes us. The levels are not very bad, but if they don't improve as we monitor Skye, she will have to get shots of erythropoietin which helps the bone marrow make more red blood cells. She'll get there. You all have my word. I am keeping a very close eye on her and any complications that may come up. I don't see this as a serious complication, please know that. Yes, it's alarming that she passed out. But the cancer did not directly cause that. She has not come out of what I am still calling a remission."

Knox exhaled in relief. And he grabbed both Afton and Laney by the shoulders in sort of a group hug.

"Thank you," Afton spoke those words, unsure if her voice would work. She was overwhelmed with emotion. *Relief and gratitude.*

"Yes! Thank you," Laney added. "When can we see her?"

"She's waiting for you now. Walk with me." He didn't plan to leave Skye's side for awhile.

Afton felt uneasy as they entered one of the cubicles in the ER. Skye had not been admitted as a patient. Dylan arranged for her to have some space away from the emergent cases. Once she saw her family, he wanted to take her home.

"Hey, look at you," Laney stated as they all crammed into the tiny cubicle. Skye was sitting on the bed dressed as if she had not been wheeled into that place on a gurney and then poked and prodded for blood withdrawal while the color eventually returned to her pale face. Afton and Knox both stayed silent.

"I am fine. Don't fuss over me," she began. "Well, *you*, can." she made direct eye contact with Dylan.

He winked at her, and replied, "I plan to."

They were an adorable pair. Afton immediately liked what she saw. Her sister was happy. She caught herself smiling at them. *They were together.* And then she again felt ridiculous and ashamed for all she had implied earlier. *To Skye, Knox was just her baby's father. Nothing more.*

"Then get me out of here. I want to see my babies!"

Knox and Dylan exchanged a look. It was as if something had been previously discussed or just simply understood between them. "Take the night to rest. Afton and I will keep them." Knox glanced at Afton, and she didn't object. It was the very least she could do right now.

"You don't have to. It's my night for them to be with me." And they had been with her. Her brother-in-law and nephews were entertaining them in the living room of their house when Skye and her sisters were in the kitchen. It was only supposed to be an hour or so of having a glass of wine and a little conversation. Instead, everything went wrong.

"We want to," Afton finally spoke. And Laney stared at her, and then back at Skye. She was the only one in the room that knew how awkward this really was between them right now.

"Okay. Thank you." Skye made fleeting eye contact between Afton and Knox. *Would they ever truly know how much she appreciated —and so desperately needed— them?* "Can I go home now?" She directed that question to Dylan.

"On one condition," he began, "after I drive you, I'll stay with you."

She suppressed a giggle. "Doctor's orders?"

"Absolutely."

They shared a smile as if no one else was in the room.

Chapter 29

Dylan was preparing to leave the ER with Skye. Knox wanted to follow Laney to her house to pick up Bella and Blair. He wasn't sure if he was going to wake them, or wait out their sleep and take them home in the early hours of the morning. The baby never slept more than four hours at a time. Afton was the only one not ready to leave, but she didn't quite know how to tell everyone to step out for a moment while she had a word with her little sister.

Skye was watching her. Afton's body language always gave her away. She looked like the wheels in her mind were turning. She had something to say. As typical of Skye, she spoke first.

"Guys, how about you all give me a minute? I'd like to talk to Afton alone." They exchanged glances. Laney was the only one who knew what was about to take place. She hoped so anyway. They needed to forgive and forget.

When it was only the two of them, she watched Afton pace at the foot of the gurney. "We never did talk about it," Skye began. "What happened between Knox and I... we just never dealt with it. I begged and pleaded with you to hear me out. To just give me the chance to explain. You ignored my messages for weeks on end. And then we finally saw each other again, at Laney's urging. You said you forgave me. You said it was going to take some time, but we would make it back to who we were together before you felt betrayed. Or, jealous." Afton opened her mouth as if she was going to shut down Skye's accusation. *She was not jealous! Or, was she?* "I think we should have talked about it. You should have allowed us to. Instead, we went on acting as if it never happened. That probably would have worked for us... if Blair Hope was not a part of our family now."

"She's a beautiful blessing to all of us," Afton spoke. She wanted to make that point very clear. This was not about that precious gift. Not *her* personally.

"I would have had a baby regardless of Knox, and your relentless urging for him to be a part of it. I told you no. I refused. I knew a bond like that would cause a rift between you and Knox, or you and me. But then I found out that I have cancer. None of us know how much time we are allocated, but when you hear the word *cancer*, you know the future is no longer your own to imagine and look forward to. The day I was diagnosed, I ended up at your house. There's just so much love there. I know it's not fair, but I made up my mind that you and Knox could raise my baby, if I shared a baby with him. And Bella too. They would be a package deal. It was the only way I could ever imagine leaving this world. Before the cancer, my greatest fear —and you already know this— was leaving her behind one day. Alone. She has Blair now. And Knox, who is like a father to her. And she has you."

There were tears rolling down her face. Sometimes Afton gave in to the emotion...no matter how much she hated to feel that vulnerable. "I don't want you to die," were the first words out of her mouth.

"I don't want to die either. I have so much to live for now. My girls. Maybe Dylan Fruend?" she smiled. "I finally have my sisters close to my heart again."

"I pushed too hard. I implied things," Afton admitted. "You're right. It bothers me that you were with Knox. No matter how many ways I tell myself that he loves me, I know that he touched you the same way. He saw your amazing body. Mine isn't so breathtaking anymore." Afton had an additional decade of wear and tear on hers. "I thought I had gotten past those feelings. This isn't about that precious baby. This is about me having to deal with sharing Knox with you. You need him, but not in the same way that I do. I realize that now. I finally opened my eyes to that tonight. You scared me. I'm still afraid that cancer will take you away from all of us. I don't want to waste time feeling negative or paranoid. I want to be who you need."

"You already are," Skye choked back her own tears. "This isn't entirely on you. Being the youngest of us girls, I always got my way. If something wasn't given to me, I found a way to take it. I should have told both of you that I was sick, instead of charging ahead with what I wanted." Skye paused. "I'm sorry." Afton continued to listen to her sincerity. "About Knox… he's a part of our family. All of us are a family. We obviously are not a typical group, but who the hell cares? I don't." Afton stifled a laugh. "Are we okay now?" Skye needed that reassurance now more than ever. This fainting episode tonight was all too real. Her health could down spiral at any given moment.

Afton stepped closer to her. "I want to be."

"Me too," Skye smiled, and held out her hand. Afton squeezed it.

"Let's get you out of here," Afton suggested. "Your doctor is waiting to take you home." They giggled. They certainly were not ordinary people in any sense of the word.

But who in the hell cared!

Chapter 30

When it seemed to be taking Afton and Skye forever to talk it out, Laney escaped to the restroom. She stood behind the closed stall door. She twisted off the cap of the flask she kept in her handbag. Typically, she added generous splashes of that vodka to her bottled water. Not tonight. She swallowed it straight, and then waited for her anxiety to subside. This was a dangerous pattern for her. She knew that, but she could not stop it. The alcohol always relieved her anxiety at first, but it also stirred parts of her brain that made her feel more anxious later. That led her to this cycle every single time. The repeated pattern of believing she needed more alcohol to relax, to feel good, and to take the edge off life. Laney left the restroom and returned to Knox waiting in the hallway.

"What's going on with those two in there?" Knox gestured toward the cubicle where Afton and Skye were having a private conversation. "You know, don't you?"

It happened to her every time. When she was drinking, her walls came down. Ask her anything, and she would tell. "They were fighting at my house earlier tonight. They were still swapping hateful words and accusations when Skye suddenly lost consciousness."

"What?" Knox was annoyed. "Why?"

"Try who," Laney spoke, feeling the effects of the alcohol buzz in her head. She laughed at her own comment. Knox was not amused. He waited for her to explain. "You, Knox. They were fighting about you. It was quite clear that Afton hasn't gotten past the night the two of you danced between the sheets." Her laughter that followed her own comment was obnoxious.

There were no sheets. There was no bed. Ugh. Knox needed to stop his thoughts. "Are you serious? I thought we had all gotten past that?"

"Apparently not."

Knox looked away. He tried to see through the curtain covering the sliding glass door of that cubicle. *Were they still at odds in there?* He wished that he could put a stop to that insanity. It certainly was time.

Knox and Afton both ended up carrying the baby and Bella out to the car, asleep. They drove home in silence, only whispering when they had to. Knox put Bella in her bed and she stayed asleep. Afton had been downstairs feeding the baby a bottle before she fell back to sleep in her arms. When Knox walked in the living room, he stared at the sight of the woman he loved holding his baby. *Would she ever really understand how much that filled his heart?* He was going to try to make her realize that tonight. He wanted to spend the rest of his life with her. And it seemed to him that she needed to be reminded of that.

Afton walked into their bedroom once Blair was sound asleep in her crib. Her feet hurt and her back ached. She wanted nothing more than to take a long, hot shower and then fall into bed. But she walked into their dark bedroom to find the fireplace lit. It was eighty-five degrees outside. Knox stood across the room from her. He had untucked his dress shirt from his pants and taken off his shoes and socks.

"What are you doing?"

"Trying to make you remember. The temperature was hot outside that night, more than a year ago, when we lit the fireplace in here for the first time. For our first time." She smiled almost in a bashful way. Beginning with their first time, he had given her a life again. A purpose to rise out of bed at the start of every new day. She hadn't forgotten. "We share a life now," he told her. "A life that has changed so much already, but I truly believe we have grown closer and stronger together. I need to know that you believe that too."

"I do," Afton spoke as if she had not needed to ponder that.

"Prove it," he told her, and his face grew serious. In just a few strides, he walked across the room and met her standing in the middle of it. She watched him bend down on one knee. Her eyes instantly clouded over with tears. Happy tears. And such joy. This man brought her all the happiness and joy that her heart could handle. More than she had ever dreamed possible. "I love you, Afton Drury. I loved you the moment I first saw you, and more every day since. I want you to be my wife. Will you marry me?" He held a small black velvet box with the most beautiful, large diamond ring sparkling back at her.

She nodded. She was not going to cry. Okay, she was crying. "Yes," she blubbered. "I'll marry you!"

Knox jumped to his feet, slipped the ring on her finger, and pulled her into his arms. He kissed her like it was the first time. Slowly, tenderly, and with heated passion.

"You planned this?' she finally caught her breath and was able to ask him that.

"I've been planning it. I wanted to wine and dine you. I should have done something more special. But I was tired of waiting for the right time. I don't want to wait anymore."

Afton laughed. "This was special, and so perfect for us. This room. That fireplace. My life changed the night you brought me upstairs to your bedroom. I felt at home then, and still do now." She wanted to freeze this moment. Knox had managed to recapture how it felt between them when all that mattered was the two of them. And that was exactly his intention. Afton needed to be reminded of his love for her. And only her.

She held up her hand to look at her engagement ring. It was unreal to her. This man, so full of goodness, loved her and wanted her. For life.

Her heart was full.

Knox took ahold of her hand *with his ring on her finger*. He softly kissed her fingers, while he kept her hand in his, and led her over to their bed.

Chapter 31

Skye unlocked her front door and Dylan stepped inside with her. The house was dark and quiet. Too quiet.

"I miss my girls," she told him.

"Get a good night's rest and bring them home tomorrow. It will do you and them so much good if you're feeling strong."

"But I don't feel awful. I did right before I passed out, but I really am fine now." She looked down at his hand. He was holding what looked like an overnight bag. He must have grabbed that from his car when they got out on the driveway. "What's this? Are you always prepared for a sleepover?"

He chuckled. "It's the doctor in me. Toothbrush, change of clothes and clean underwear."

"You really don't have to stay all night with me." She said the words, but gosh she wanted him to.

"Is it alright if I want to? I promised your family that I would keep a close eye on you. I want to be here for you, Skye, if that's what you want too."

She reached for his hand and walked him through her house. She flipped on a few lights to lead their way. They stood upstairs in the hallway where there were four bedrooms. Three were spoken for, and one was a guest room. She led him there. "You can put your things in there. There's a private bathroom too."

"So, I'm a guest in your home tonight?" he teased her. This time he led her, as they made their way into that guest room, and he initiated for her to sit down beside him on the end of the bed.

"Talk to me. If you're afraid, I want to ease those fears. I know being in the ER tonight made your mind reel."

"I don't want to think about what could be happening inside of my body right now. I can't let myself go there. I am obsessed with the word remission… with the prospect of staying in that place forever. Is that even possible? I think we both know it's not. Dylan, there's so much uncertainty with me. Do you really want to put yourself right here?" Skye put her hand over her heart. God, she hoped that he did. For reasons unknown, he was in her life. And there were times she believed his optimism kept her strong. But she knew that alone could not keep her healthy forever. She had to give him the opportunity to back away from this before it would hurt too much.

"I'm overly obsessed with that word, too," he smiled. He didn't know if it was possible to remain in remission indefinitely. Anything was medically probable, he had learned from experience. He ruled nothing out. But he also never gave anyone false hope. "I appreciate you giving me the chance to show myself to the door," he looked deeply into her eyes. She was sitting right beside him. Their legs were touching. Their hands were on their respective laps. "But I'm not interested in walking away to save myself from the uncertainty, as you put it. Do any of us know what is around the corner in our lives? No. So, you see, I'm no different than you."

"You're not sick," she was quick to call him out on his words.

"You just told me that you feel perfectly fine, so let's focus on that, shall we? I want to be with you." *In sickness and in health, if it had to be that way.* "When I am not with you, I'm thinking about you. That's not something I want to walk away from, if you feel the same."

She touched him first. Her open palm was on the side of his smooth-shaven face. Even after all day long, there was no stubble on his soft skin. "I feel the same," she spoke in barely a whisper. She felt tears on her face as he pressed his lips to hers. Their worlds collided. And suddenly the apprehension and the reluctance faded away. If that's the way it was going to be with him, Skye would never again give him the chance to walk away from her. She already loved him. She felt it in her soul when he looked at her. And when he touched her.

She tore herself away from him. But only momentarily. And then she led him by the hand, across the hall to her bedroom. He wasn't going to be a merely guest in her house after all.

They laid together on her king-size bed with coral-colored bedding. She had the fancy dust ruffle that bordered the base of the bed, the pillow shams on top of the matching duvet, all of it. It was a woman's bedroom. Dylan smiled to himself. There was so much about her he wanted to know, and learn, and be a part of. Her face was in his hands. They were going to take this slow. And savor every second of being together, like this, for the first time. It never felt this way for her before. Skye was always in love with the mere idea of falling in love. It had just never happened.

"I feel like I should say something," she spoke, her lips were just inches from his.

"Right now?" he chuckled.

"Yes, right now," she playfully mimicked him, and he snuck a soft kiss on her lips. "I've never done things this way before. I fell for you while I was sitting on exam table paper," she laughed out loud. "Then you courted me like a schoolgirl, kissing me until I was breathless and then leaving me longing for more. I think we both are past due, to be together like this. I want to make love with you."

"Is this the part where I say something too?" he teased her. And then she stole a kiss from his lips. "I fell for you, too. And restraining from making love to you all these weeks has been one cold shower after another." She giggled, and he teasingly rolled his eyes. "I don't know if there is a timetable for this, and honestly I don't care. I want to say it. I want to tell you, before I make love to you, exactly how I feel. I love you, Skye Gallant. I love how you talk, the way your bottom sways in your tight pants when you walk. I love that you are an ambitious, successful woman, and a brave and loving mother. I love how loud you are, and you don't even care who's around. I love how you have to blurt out exactly what you are thinking before anyone else has a chance to speak at all. I also love knowing that there are things about you that I have yet to learn."

"I wanted to say it first," she smiled with her eyes. "I love you, Dylan Fruend. So very much. You make me want to be a better person. I feel your positivity and your strength. You're smart and strong, kind and compassionate, and so incredibly sexy. I'm so ready to learn more about you, too."

And this was the part where they needed to stop talking.

He pulled her close to him and kissed her full on the lips. She immediately deepened that kiss. Their passion could escalate from zero to eighty with just one kiss. Their desire to be together, to see and to feel each other's bodies, was mounting. She undid the buttons on his dress shirt, quickly, one after another. She helped him out of it. She ran her fingers across his broad, tight chest. He took off the sleeveless scoop-neck shirt she wore. He looked down at her lacy pale pink bra. He touched her. He kissed her hard on the mouth, made his way down her neck, to her collarbone, and then lower. She reached behind her back and undid the clasp of her bra. Her full breasts were free for him. He traced her nipples with his fingers and then met his mouth with each one. He took his time. She arched her back, moaned his name. Their bare chests were pressed together. Flesh on flesh. And they needed more. Skye reached for his belt buckle when he slid his hand into the now undone zipper of her short white shorts. He felt her through the lacy underwear that he already knew matched her bra. She opened for him, and he ached to remove her shorts and panties. He too got out of his pants and underwear. It was time to have nothing between them. She touched him. He groaned. He closed his eyes. He opened them again. He couldn't wait much longer. But he wanted to. He needed to savor this woman. And all the time they had together.

They kissed until they were breathless, while touching each other again and again. He moved between her legs. He wanted to know every inch of her body. He discovered exactly where she wanted him. He pleasured her until she found her release. And he was there, right there, to devour her. She was the sexiest, most passionate woman he had ever touched. He straddled her. She guided him with her hands. She moved and made her way down to take him into her mouth, briefly but seductively, as if she was priming him. He took it all in. And then he let her guide him to her opening. He pushed himself inside. Nothing ever felt so right, or more perfect. He rocked over her. She wrapped her never-ending legs around his back. They found a rhythm that was made for them. She cried out. Well, more like, she screamed. Loudly! She was on the verge of ecstasy again. *Yes, yes, yes!* His thrusts became harder and more desperate, until they became one. Body and soul.

Chapter 32

Laney and Brad settled into bed soon after Afton and Knox picked up the girls and took them home. Laney turned on her side to face Brad, who was lying on his back. The room was dark, but she could make out his face. He was the most familiar human being to her. She knew every inch of him. She knew that once he fell asleep on his back, he would subconsciously turn to his right side for his best sleep. He slept on one flat, firm pillow while she needed two soft ones. He liked very little to cover him and always pushed the sheet and duvet down to his waist. She preferred to be chin deep in both of those. But what she needed most —aside from the perfect pillows or the comfort of her entire body being covered— was him. Brad was her comfort. Her constant.

He was unusually quiet, so Laney broke that silence before they drifted off to sleep. "I know it was out of the norm for you and the boys tonight, but you really saved us when you offered to watch the little ones." They didn't have anyone else to depend on, other than the daycare both girls attended. Brad had rescued them.

"Oh it was fine. They mostly slept. I think the boys enjoyed it more than they would admit." He chuckled in the dark. He was still on his back though, and their bodies were not touching. He felt distant to her. She reached for him, and he didn't respond, physically.

"We should get some sleep," he said.

She couldn't remember a time ever when he had rejected her. Tears sprung to her eyes. Something was wrong. "Brad. Talk to me. Are you upset?" She wondered if he felt left out, or pushed aside, tonight. That wasn't at all like him though.

"You were drinking tonight," he stated as a matter of fact.

"Yeah, we had some wine here before Skye passed out and panic set in for all of us."

"I mean after that. I don't know, at the hospital? In the car? You carry that damn flask everywhere you go." The tone of his voice did not change. He was aware of their boys down the hall, and didn't want them to overhear him.

"I did have a few sips of vodka to calm my nerves. Jesus, Brad. My sister could have had a relapse tonight. We could have been given terrible news."

"You make excuses all the time. You need to take the edge off. You want to chase away the anxiety that built up after a long day at school. Liam is stressing you out. Luke got another sports injury. When will it stop? Where will you draw the line and finally stop needing alcohol to function?"

His words hurt her. She now turned away from him and was also flat on her back. She couldn't remember a time when they felt this far apart lying right beside each other. Inches from touching. Yet terribly distant. "I'm sorry," was all she said.

"Are you? I don't believe that you are, because when we are remorseful, we change. We make it better. We learn and we grow from our mistakes and the challenges that life sometimes forces at us. We don't keep repeating the same drunken pattern over and over again." He paused, as if he was working up the courage to say more. "I'm done," she heard her husband —the only man she ever loved— say.

Laney wanted to ask him what he just said, or what he meant by those words, but she was too afraid. Because she already feared she knew. She was so taken aback by his words that she stayed silent for the longest time. And then finally, Brad heard her say, "You love me. You are not done."

He swallowed hard. There was a knot in his throat the size of the baseball he and the boys still liked to throw around in the backyard. A tear escaped from the corner of his eye. "I do love you. I always have, and I always will. But you need help, Lane. And until you choose to get it, I want you to live somewhere else. I can't be apart from the boys. And they don't need to keep seeing you like this, on some sort of downward spiral. This isn't you.

And we are so far from being us. I won't settle for as broken as we are right now."

"You're telling me to go?" she was instantly angry.

"There's a facility in Minneapolis, it's an addiction treatment center called the Eden House. There's a six-week rehab program. All you have to do is go there. I can drive you there. Whatever you want. Just please agree to get some help."

Laney had tears rolling down her cheeks, off her face, and onto her pillow. She tried to stifle her sobs. She didn't want him to know she was falling apart. The worst of this was this ultimatum he gave her was an impossible choice. She couldn't lose him, but she wasn't courageous enough to give up drinking. She needed both to survive. *The love of her life. And alcohol.* Without one or the other, Laney believed her life would be over.

"I can't believe what you are asking of me," she told him. It broke his heart to hear the sadness and the disappointment in her voice. But he had no choice. If he didn't do this, he would never have a fighting chance to get his Laney back.

Brad turned his back to her after he told her she could decide in the morning where she wanted to go. Either way, she needed to pack her bags.

Laney stared at the ceiling nearly all night long, not having slept at all. And finally, she made her decision in the early morning hours.

About the Author

This story, *As We Are,* continued with the intricate and unpredictable lives of the Gallant sisters. Laney could not handle the pressures of life and gradually turned to alcohol as a buffer. Her struggle will continue in Book 3 of this series. Will she finally overcome her addiction in order to save her marriage? Brad believes his ultimatum is the only thing that can reach her and force her into sobriety. But sadly, he's proven wrong when their lives take an unexpected turn.

Skye will continue to raise her girls, and Dylan Fruend will begin to fit comfortably into all of their lives. The question of whether or not the myeloma will stay in remission is a huge focus of the third and final book in this series. Expect anything as this story continues and then concludes. Honestly, I still do not know how this particular storyline will play out. I do believe there is a reason that Skye and her doctor crossed paths and fell in love.

Jess Robertson has fallen into an old pattern that could get her into more trouble than she's ever seen. Her late husband's cousin, Patrick, becomes yet another man obsessed with having her in his life. Afton again will be her biggest support system. The strength of their bond will remain stronger than the truth, as they continue to share the secret of Sam's demise. But do all secrets eventually come out?

And finally, Afton and Knox will continue to face joy and pain. They were the couple that started this series, and they will play a huge role in how it ends.

Writing my first trilogy has been incredibly challenging and also rewarding. I take the development of all of my characters to heart every single time. I am in love with these characters and I'm rooting for all of them. Stay with me as I write *For Reasons Unknown,* which will be Book 3 of the Stronger than Truth series. Look for a release date in October/November of 2019.

As always, thank you for reading!

Love,

Lori Bell

Made in the USA
Columbia, SC
07 August 2019